S
TRANQUILITY

DRAGON DESCENDANTS
BOOK 1

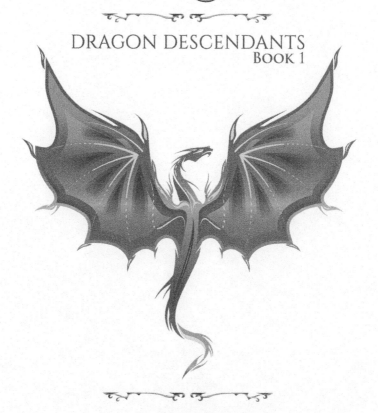

FROM
USA TODAY BESTSELLING AUTHOR
J.L WEIL

CONTENTS

DRAGON DESCENDANTS

A REVERSE HAREM SERIES

COPYRIGHTS

Copyright © 2018 J.L. Weil. All rights reserved.
ISBN-13: 978-1725949492

Edited by Allisyn Ma.
Proofread by Stephany Wallace
Cover Design by Alerim. All Rights Reserved.
Interior Design and Formatting by Stephany Wallace. All Rights Reserved.

A Dark Magick Publishing publication, Aug 2018
www.jlweil.com

DRAGON DESCENDANTS

A REVERSE HAREM SERIES

WRITTEN BY J.L. WEIL

DRAGON DESCENDANTS

A REVERSE HAREM SERIES

ABOUT STEALING TRANQUILITY

Get ready to meet Jase, Kieran, Zade, and Issik—the last dragon descendants.

Stealing Tranquility will transport fans of *Twilight*, *A Shade of Vampire*, and *Shadowhunters* to an enchanted world unlike any other . . .

Olivia Campbell's life gets turned upside down when her mother suddenly passes away. Left with only a stepdad who despises her, she turns to the streets. Penniless and alone in the Chicago winter, how much worse can it get?

She is about to find out.

A chance encounter with a stranger who has the most breathtaking violet eyes changes her world. Just a warm smile and a quick flash of dimples is all that it takes to capture her interest in Jase Dior. Olivia wonders if her luck has finally returned.

She soon finds out that Jase collects things—pretty girls to be precise. A glimpse of her sultry honey hair in an alley excites him. He must have her. And he isn't taking no for an answer.

Jase sweeps Olivia off the streets to the Veil Isles—a mystical and hidden land uncharted by any mortal and ruled by the only dragon coven left in the world.

What the hell did she get herself into?

Four dragons.
One headstrong heroine.
And a reverse-harem fantasy romance that could change the fate of a dying race.
Prepare for a unique spin on the lore you love and an adventure that is as thrilling as it is unexpected.

*Recommended for ages 17+ due to language and sexual content.

DEDICATION

This book is for readers.
I wouldn't be able to do any of this without you!
I FLOVE you!

ACKNOWLEDGMENTS

First and foremost, I want to thank Stephany Wallace for being more than an incredible PA and editor, but also being my cheerleader and friend. I wouldn't get through my edits without those comments that make me lol.

Another huge thank you to Allisyn, who constantly helps me grow in my skills as a writer. I really do take all your notes to heart, even if it seems as if I'd forgotten them.

I want to give a big shoutout to the YA Vets. You know who you are. This group is a resource I can't do without. Muawah!

And as always, a massive thank you to the readers and reviewers. You guys give me the encouragement to keep doing this and making me believe in my dreams. I FLOVE all of you!

My feet pounded the pavement as I ran down the street. A warm pizza box bounced in my hands while my Converse crunched pebbles, empty soda cans, and discarded fast food wrappers. I probably shouldn't be running. It wasn't my forte. Any second, I was positive I would do a face-plant, and end up losing my first meal in days.

"Come back, you little thief!"

Thief? Okay, so technically I did steal a pizza, but in my defense, I was starving, and this was about survival.

The cook chasing me was bound to run out of steam soon. I hoped. The last thing I needed was to get caught.

Pushing myself, I bolted down Elm Avenue like my hair was on fire, dodging a couple walking their dog. I turned the corner and a gust of wind slapped me in the face. Damn. If this took much longer, my pizza would be cold.

"I'm calling the cops!" he yelled.

Go for it. Good luck finding me. I would take my chances and called bs on his threat.

I knew the difference between right and wrong, and stealing was wrong, but sometimes, you needed to break the law to live, or starve to death. And I wasn't ready to die.

This wasn't the first time I'd stolen a meal, and honestly, I doubted it would be my last. When I came across the restaurant earlier, I had stopped and glanced longingly at the filled booths, seeing the happy faces as the patrons stuffed their bellies full of garlic breadsticks, and deep-dish pizza. At that moment, I would have killed for a hot slice of sausage with extra cheese, loaded with tomato sauce. My stomach rumbled (angry with me), telling me I needed to find food sooner than later.

That's when the plan had been born. Over the last few weeks, I'd become quite skilled at being invisible, and taking what I wanted. Wallets. Clothes. And pizza.

I had scampered down the pizzeria's alley, seeing the back door slightly ajar. From inside, I'd heard voices and the smells of baked dough, zesty tomato sauce, and Italian herbs. Peeking around the door, I had spotted an open box with a fresh-out-of-the-oven pizza sitting on the end of a metal counter. All I had thought was *Jackpot!*

My triumph had been short-lived, unfortunately.

Looking left and right, I had tiptoed inside, keeping below the counter. There had been a guy opening one of the many ovens and another spinning a ball of dough in the air. Both of them had seemed too occupied to notice me. Quickly, I snatched the box and backed out the way I had come in.

"Hey!" a voice had called behind me.

I hadn't bothered to look, and just started running, the pizza box tucked under my arm. It hadn't been a very thought-out decision, but rarely any of mine were. Stealing wasn't something I wanted on my record.

Hell. I didn't want a record at all.

At just a few months shy of eighteen, I would be shoved into a foster home or juvie, and I'd rather live on the streets. My legs burned, and my lungs ached from the chill, but I

2

pressed on, glancing over my shoulder to judge how much distance I had gained. Not enough.

For a cook, the guy was persistent—not that I knew a lot of cooks, just what I'd seen on TV, but most of them didn't strike me as a *long-distance running* type of guys.

Just my luck that this chef would be the exception.

Taking the next right, I cut the corner sharply, and the bottom of my worn-out shoes skidded over loose rock. My hands flailed in the air as I lost my balance. Shit. This was it. The face-plant was imminent.

By an act of God, I managed to stay on my feet, keep the pizza in my hand, and regain my composure. *Smooth move, Olivia.* I took off down Oglesby Street.

"I better not see your face again!" the cook screamed, finally giving up. He stood panting at the corner.

Yes! Victory is mine.

A smile crossed my lips when I hooked a left around the corner, but I didn't ease up on my pace for another five minutes and refrained from jumping in the air. Being homeless stunk, and I wasn't just talking about my body odor. Being homeless in Chicago was plain insanity.

An icy breeze whipped through my hoodie, sending a thousand tiny pinpricks over my flesh. I huddled up against a brick wall, the smell of pizza stirring up hunger pangs that assaulted my belly.

I crouched in a corner behind a dumpster in an empty alley near the local college, digging into the pizza box with a sigh of pleasure. I savored the taste of sweet basil tomato sauce and mozzarella cheese, burning it to memory. This was a moment I didn't want to forget.

I swallowed, positive I'd died and gone to heaven.

When was the last time I had pizza?

Months?

I couldn't be certain. Hell, I didn't even know what time it was, what day, or if I would survive the night. What I did know was I was going to feast like a king and then find somewhere warm to stay before I froze to death. The boogers in my nose already had ice crystals forming on them.

On nights like this, it was hard to forget how my life had ended up so pitifully. It was never supposed to be like this, not for me, but fate had a way of throwing you curveballs.

Like the day I found out Mom was killed in a car crash. After she passed, her loser husband—not my father—had decided he no longer wanted a kid, especially an angry and lost one. Denny had his own life, his own plans, and those didn't include me. Not that I cared. He was an asshat. I didn't need him. That had been my mantra since the stepfather-of-the-year had kicked me out two months ago. I'd been on my own ever since.

My real father split when I was a baby. Mom sure knew how to pick them.

Good riddance.

I didn't need a daddy figure anyway.

My mother had been beautiful, silky honey hair that shone in the sunlight, curves that turned men's heads, and aqua eyes that glittered like the ocean. Everyone had said we looked like sisters, twins even, but our personalities couldn't have been more different. For all her flaws, I loved her immensely. We had been partners, best friends, and I missed her something fierce. She might have been flighty in love, but as a mother, she was everything a girl could ask for.

I was determined to not be so unlucky in love, which was why I planned to never fall into it. I was protecting my heart. Mine had bled enough.

After Mom's accident, my life as I knew it was over, but I never imagined it would be this bad. I blamed my stepfather for everything. He didn't even really qualify as one. The two of us never saw eye-to-eye. Mom had an older sister, but I knew very little about her and even less about my real father and his family. It was just me, myself, and I.

Those first few weeks after Mom passed were the worst. I'd never felt so alone in my life, and if it hadn't been for my best friend, Staci, I don't think I would have gotten through it. Staci and I were friends at first sight. Her personality matched her wild wardrobe, which looked like Katy Perry's stylist had sex with Marilyn Manson's makeup artist and Staci was the result. Her pink short hair, heavy eyeliner, black nail polish, pink boots, and tight jeans completed her everyday look, and yet she managed to appear adorable.

Staci had begged me to come stay with her, and as much as I wanted to, I knew her mom couldn't afford to care for me. She had her hands full, working two jobs to support Staci, and her younger brother, Aiden. I refused to burden my best friend. If I could get a job and contribute, that would be another story, which was what I would do first thing Monday morning—job hunt.

And for tonight, I would just try to survive.

As I downed my second slice, a mouse scampered out of its hiding spot, and stared up at me. I swallowed my initial squeak with a bite of pizza. "Hey, little guy, you hungry?"

Breaking off a hunk of crust, I dropped it onto the ground. Pipsqueak scurried over, and grabbed the offering in his two tiny hands, nibbling with an intensity that I understood far too well.

"Not bad, huh?"

Holy shit. I'd been reduced to talking to the local street rodents. At least he had better table manners than Denny. I'd take a dozen mice over him any day of the week.

I polished off half the pizza—my first real meal in two days—my belly felt fully satisfied for the time being. Licking the last bit of sauce from my fingers, I stood up, gathering the other half of the pizza as a blast of wind bit straight into me.

Ugh. This sucks. I cursed Denny to seven different kinds of hell as I shivered my ass off, but I didn't regret standing up to my stepdad. Screw him. He was a piece of trash.

Winter reared its ugly head, and the bone-chilling wind made me want to huddle forever in my hoodie, and never take it off. Leaning against the wall, my mind wandered to the days when I used to hang out with Staci. I missed her and her off-the-wall sense of humor. She worried about me... the only person who did.

Checking my phone I exhaled. No messages. It was hard not to feel unloved at the moment and utterly alone in the world. I didn't expect her to blow up my phone every five minutes, but the occasional *are you okay?* text would be nice.

The coolness of the bricks reached me when I rested my head back, and glanced up at the charming, and historical Brentley University. Remembering the application I had completed to attend this school, it was hard to realize my dreams had been swept away. I had left it sitting on my desk at the house Denny now occupied alone. It was probably crumbled and in the trash now, just like my future.

Throwing my backpack onto my shoulders, I moseyed to the end of the alley, gaining a clear picture of the campus courtyard. It was sad, but I used to sit on the benches, watching the throngs of students come and go from the dorms and classes, picturing myself among them.

Someday, I promised myself. Someday I would go to college, but first I needed to figure out how to finish high school, and I couldn't forget about that J-O-B.

A gaggle of giggles interrupted my drifting thoughts, and drew my attention to a group of college students whispering in a circle. I rolled my eyes, glad I'd never been one of those annoying girls, but still, curiosity got the best of me while my gaze followed theirs across campus.

Keeping myself partially hidden in the dark alley, I glanced at the parking lot, seeing a sporty black car. Leaning on the sleek vehicle was a tall, attractive man. His legs were crossed at the ankles, as he shot an award-winning grin at his fan club.

Leif Lexington. He had been a senior last year at my school and was smoldering hot with an ego the size of the Sears Tower. The pizza threatened to come back up. Guys like Leif made me sick. So what if he drove a stellar car, had perfect blond hair, and sexy scruff? I found it freaky. No one could be that perfect.

What a douche-sicle.

The clique of girls might as well drop their panties. Cringe.

Leif forked his fingers through his hair, giving it that messy, I-just-woke-up-like-this look that he probably spent hours perfecting. I swore I heard a chorus of sighs, even from my hiding spot.

The gag reflex started in the back of my throat. It was a train wreck I couldn't stop watching, like reality TV.

One of his groupies got the lady balls to approach him, her heeled boots clattering on the pavement as she strutted to the parking lot. A seductive smirk coated her cherry lips. Leif reached into the back pocket of his tattered black jeans —that probably cost more than the entire wardrobe hanging in my old closet—pulled out a lighter, and a small red box of Marlboros.

Gross.

How could they think that was hot?

With a flick of his thumb, the flame on the lighter caught, casting a soft glow over his flawless face, while he put a slim white cigarette into his mouth. He cupped the dancing fire with his hand, bending his face to catch the tip as he sucked in, sharpening his cheekbones.

If he could see me now, I doubted he would recognize me. I was repulsed to admit that at one time Leif had briefly dated Staci, which could account for 90 percent of my dislike for the guy. To this day, I still don't know what my best friend saw in him, but I guess she had wanted to give dating Mr. Popular a shot, just to say she had.

As if his nose was itching, Leif's sparkly silver eyes whisked to the alley, catching a glimpse of me staring at him. The corners of his mouth twitched. There was something aloof and pompous about the slight tilt of his lips. I jerked back, sinking farther into the darkness, and out of his eyesight.

Color heightened my cheeks. *Crap. Had he seen me?*

The last thing I wanted was rumors spread about me at school. Leif had a younger brother, and at my high school, gossip spread like cancer.

Worry ran through me. *I need to find something better than this.* Living on the streets couldn't be my life.

The girl with mile-long legs reached Leif, taking his attention, but not before I caught the sneer on his lips.

Ugh.

I pressed my back against the wall, arguing with myself. *Don't do it, Olivia. Just walk away.* But it was as if I was possessed. Turning against the brick building, I inched forward, taking another peek. Legs laughed at something Leif said, tossing her ebony hair over her shoulder, and then she placed a flirty hand on his chest.

I snorted.

What they were saying wasn't clear, but it didn't really matter; their body language said it all. Wariness held me back. Something in Leif's gaze made me shudder. He was a tad too controlled. Edging along the wall, I moved farther away from the couple, no longer interested in taking a trip down memory lane, and what he had done to my best friend.

My gaze dropped to my phone for the umpteenth time—nothing new. I noticed the date was the winter solstice. In high school, I'd been fascinated with astronomy. The beginning of winter was here... and the beginning of death for everything else. The plants, the trees, all of it would become stagnant, and here in Chicago, winter wasn't some little event; it lasted months.

A flutter drew my eyes to a shadowed corner near the dumpster. As I grew closer, I noticed it was just a discarded magazine, the pages flapping in the wind. My fingers grazed its pages when I bent down to pick it up. I could use some reading material—a form of entertainment to pass the long night ahead—but first, I needed to find a bathroom. That was one of the things you never thought about before becoming homeless—how difficult it was to do something as simple as pee.

Scooping up the gossip tabloid, a lock of blonde hair fell over my eyes, partially impairing my vision. I stood up and turned the corner, not thinking about where I was going, and smacked into a wall, spilling my pizza. I was always doing crap like that. Being graceful wasn't one of my redeeming qualities.

Son of a bitch. The last thing I need is a bloody nose.

Correction: It wasn't a wall. Just a guy with abs of steel, and I had barreled straight into him. Besides losing my next meal, the collision caused my bag to slip off my shoulder and on to a slice of cheese pizza. *Freaking wonderful.*

"Maybe watch where you're going..."

The rest of my snappy retort got stuck in my throat when my eyes slammed into his. I immediately shut my mouth, and stared into the prettiest eyes I'd ever seen. Bold and bright, they were an unusual violet color. My gaze roamed over the rest of his face, intrigue sucking me in. His cheeks jutted out at sharp angles that led to a defined jaw and full lips, which quirked at the corners.

What did he find so amusing?

I bristled.

I didn't care how jaw dropping he was. The look in his stunning eyes made me uncomfortable—their intensity over-whelming. Why was he staring at me? If he was expecting an apology, he would be sorely disappointed.

The guy towered over me, and my neck cramped from looking up at him. For some reason, he took a step toward me, forcing my back against the damp concrete wall.

The first strings of fear wrapped around my heart. Something in his eyes had my internal alarm going off. This guy was dangerous. He continued to scrutinize me, and my eyes shifted, taking in the rest of his appearance.

He had an obvious love for black. His dark pressed suit with a white cotton T-shirt underneath made him appear older than his smooth face. He couldn't have been more than a year or two older than me, which made me think he was a trust fund baby. An influential and dominating presence emanated from him, reeking of trouble.

His midnight brow lifted—the same shade as his wind-blown hair. "Are you okay?" His voice was cool and silky. It had a calming effect on my ears, almost hypnotic.

Did he just say something? I shook my head. "What?"

Shifting his stance, he allowed me a smidgen of space, his gaze still relentless. It felt as if he was dissecting me bit by bit with the ferocity of his eyes. I found them mesmerizing and difficult to look away.

"You know, you can stop staring now," I ground out. I needed to keep his gaze focused on my eyes, my lips, my boobs, any part of me that was distracting, so my hands were free to slip into his pockets. And voilà. Hopefully, I was bit richer tonight.

"And miss seeing your pretty face?"

Damn, did the sound of his voice have to be so rich and sensual? He grinned, revealing deep dimples on either cheek. His face now an inch from mine.

From this angle, I spotted a black leather wallet peeking out of his inside jacket pocket. To distract him further, I pushed his chest and, at the same time, I slipped his wallet into my coat pocket, and then folded my arms, needing some sort of defense from his body. Was he flirting with *me*?

"I'm not a hooker, if that's what you're looking for."

His lips thinned, no longer amused. "I'm not, but I am looking for someone."

"Uh, I'm definitely not her. So..." I hoped he would get out of my way and let me pass. I was wrong. What was with people? Did I have a tattoo on my forehead saying "Sucker"? My mouth started flapping before I could stop myself. "Um, do you think you could step back? I really need to pee." *Classy, Olivia. You run into a hot, rich guy and all you can think to say is "I have to pee"?*

Ugh. I wanted to crawl under the nearest bench. Heat crawled over my neck. I shouldn't have been surprised by his reaction, but I was as his lips curled.

"What are you doing out here alone?" he asked, ignoring my need for space. His eyes suddenly took on a new interest in me.

Major warning bells went off, and I scrambled to come up with something that would ward off any seedy ideas. "For your information, I'm not alone. I'm actually on my way to the dorms, which, last I checked, isn't a crime. I'm meeting my huge—I'm talking massive—boyfriend. Like he has muscles for days." Okay, I might have laid that on a little thick. He probably didn't believe me.

He leaned down, the scent of him assaulting my senses, like the sea after a thunderstorm, and I gulped. Why did he have to smell so freaking good? It derailed my train of thought. "Is that so?" he challenged me.

"If you make another move toward me, I'm punching you in the dick." Defense 101: Hit a guy where it hurts, and then run.

He chuckled, and my hands balled into fists. "This has been interesting." Those violet eyes bored into mine, and he lifted a hand as if to touch my cheek.

I should have made good on my threat, instead of just standing there like I'd never seen a guy before. My behavior was odd, but then again, so was this entire encounter.

I held my breath, waiting.

He dropped his hand, the muscles in his body suddenly tightening. Something other than me had his back prickling up, and I was curious what it was. Running a hand through his hair, those piercing eyes returned to mine. "Not possible," he muttered.

For a paralyzing moment, I thought I had been caught red-handed. Anxiously, I tucked my honey blonde hair behind my ears to keep it from hanging in my face and raised a brow. *What is he mumbling about?*

With an expression I couldn't pin, he turned and walked off. No apology. No "it was nice meeting you." Just a cold shoulder and a bizarre meeting.

I watched him strut across the perfectly manicured court-yard with purposeful strides. Wow. I was just going to pretend the last ten minutes had never happened, except my mind was plagued with questions.

What had he meant by "not possible"?

Who was he?

Where was he going?

What was his name?

I hated mysteries, and that guy oozed unanswered questions.

He never bothered to look back, and for some inexplic-able reason, it irked me. One thing was clear, I needed to get off the streets and the hell out of Chicago. There was nothing holding me here, other than Staci, but she would be headed to college soon.

With a sigh of regret, I gave Brentley University one last glimpse, and went in search of a bathroom.

My mind mulled over everything I'd lost as I walked— Mom, my home, my friends, all sense of love and stability.

No wonder I'd become so cynical. The measly amount of money in my bank account wouldn't last longer than a few days, and I was saving it to get out of here. California sounded heavenly right about now. Warm, sandy beaches. Bountiful opportunities. And miles away from Denny.

How could I say no?

Shifting my bag that housed everything I owned higher on my shoulder, I walked toward a building on the edge of campus. I jogged up the steps, pushing the door open to the commons of Cummings Hall. The ladies' room was to the left. I quickly took care of my bladder, and went to wash my hands, splashing warm water on my face. In the side pocket of my bag, I dug out my hairbrush and ran it through my snarled hair.

Feeling halfway normal, I stared at my reflection. Who would have ever thought the clumsy, sassy girl from Wrigleyville would end up here? Not me. Not in a million years. I would have laughed in their faces.

My aqua eyes were tired and puffy. No amount of cream would fix these bad boys, but a pillow top mattress and a solid ten hours of sleep would do wonders. The only thing saving me from looking like a zombie was my thick, dark eyelashes. I never had to wear mascara. The dusting of freckles sprinkled over the bridge of my nose had started to fade as winter approached.

I fitted a beanie over my hair to prevent the wind from knotting it, and my keep ears warm. Digging into my coat pocket, I pulled out the sucker's wallet and fumbled through the slots.

Son of a bitch.

There was nothing. No credit cards. No cash. Not even an ID. Who the hell carries around an empty wallet? A ghost, that's who, or someone with something to hide. And the mysterious stranger seemed to have plenty to hide. I still didn't know his name. Disappointed, I tossed the black leather billfold into the garbage, cursing my luck. I should have gone for the watch.

Sighing, I gathered my bag, and set out to find a cozy spot I could curl up in for the night. The train station was always an option, but I risked being kicked out by security, and I wasn't in the mood to deal with authority figures. My other option was an abandoned warehouse behind the convenience store that had come in handy, and I had often made it my own little sanctuary at night.

I hauled ass down the stone steps of Cummings Hall—not very gracefully I might add—when a shiver wracked my body, as a jolt of icy wind whipped through me. Leif and his harem were nowhere in sight. Stealing a glance over my shoulder, I saw the sidewalks were vacant, but a sudden flight response rose up inside me. With each step, I couldn't shake the instinct, and instead of ignoring the feeling, I took a quick turn toward the courtyard—away from the campus buildings behind me. While trekking across the street, some jackass honked from his Mercedes, and I flipped him off, jumping onto the sidewalk. Chicago traffic was the absolute worst.

It was only a few blocks' walk, but as I passed Lou's Quick Mart, the prickly sensation of being followed increased tenfold. I turned my head around for another peek. Again, no one there. I bolted.

This was definitely one of my not very thought-out decisions, but I also didn't want to get killed tonight. Better safe than sorry. If I was wrong, no harm. Sure, I might feel silly afterward, and have a quick laugh, but I would be safe.

The sound of footsteps pounding behind me told me I'd made the right choice. I amplified my speed, flying over the grass. My Converse sunk into the damp dirt, and I lost my beanie in the process. Strands of my hair flung in my face as I ran. It didn't take long for my legs to burn and my lungs to ache from the exertion, but I pushed myself. Blood rushed to my cheeks as my heart quickened.

Terror clamped down on my chest and settled. Knowing this could end badly, like really bad for me, I refused to think of who was chasing me or what they wanted. Damn those horror books I'd been obsessed with in high school. My imagination was getting the best of me.

Money?

Rape?

Torture?

Slavery?

A million horrible scenarios raced through my head, clouding my ability to keep my wits sharp—a huge mistake.

"Who the hell is following me?" I asked myself as confusion set in beside the fear. The only thing I was certain of was I needed to get somewhere public at record speeds.

I cut the corner toward the multistory buildings, but realized my mistake, having turned right instead of left. I stared at a dead end alley.

Smart move, Olivia. Now what?

"Shit. Shit. Shit," I muttered out loud, trying to gather my thoughts through the slick feeling of terror. It gripped me, and for a second, I was afraid I would cower into a ball in the middle of the street.

I jerked around, hoping I had enough of a lead to back-track before my stalker cornered me. No go.

A shadow stood in the mouth of the alley, blocking the exit. From the size of his form, it was a man... a very big man.

Trapped, I released a soft whimper. My breath came out in a cloud in front of my face. *What do I do?* Did I even have options at this point? What could I do besides cry for help, and hope someone came to my rescue?

I didn't like my odds. Not at this time of night or in this part of town. Everyone was in their dorms with the music turned up, and people were laughing, drinking. Who was going to hear the cries of a desperate girl?

I opened my mouth to scream, and that was when I heard a familiar voice. Someone I'd only met a short while ago, but was unlikely to forget.

"Just the girl I was hoping to run into," a deep and rich voice said from the darkness.

Son of a bitch.

I was going to cause him bodily harm for real this time.

The very last person I ever thought I'd see again, stood in front of me in all his pompous glory—the jackass with the dreamy eyes and sinful dimples, who had almost mowed me down in the last alley we'd shared. The one I had stolen the empty wallet from earlier. What were the freaking odds?

Pretty slim, I thought, unless he'd been following me.

But why would he do that? Why would he care about a wallet with nothing in it?

"You!" I accused him, a feeling of anger engulfing me, and giving me a dose of boldness. "You've been following me. Why?" I demanded, as my eyes bore into his First rule of being a thief: never admit to what you've done.

My mysterious stalker lifted a brow, his form dwarfing the entrance of the alley. Words couldn't do justice to how striking his face was—a truly unearthly beauty. His violet eyes were a stark contrast to his fair skin. "You intrigue me."

I wanted to berate him for scaring me half to death. I didn't need any more nightmares in my life. "The laws of nature intrigue me. Literature intrigues me. Stars intrigue me. But following people down dark alleys doesn't intrigue me. I think you might need some new hobbies. Stalking is creepy."

"It wasn't my intent to frighten you," he said, a smile playing on his lips.

He needed to stop doing that—flashing those dimples at me. I didn't like the way my belly flip-flopped. "Why don't I believe you?" I shifted my feet, dying to run again. The dreamy stranger made me wary.

"Because you're smart. What's your name?"

His voice sounded closer than it had before, but I hadn't even seen him move. I glared. "Sorry, I don't think names are necessary. I've got places to be." I started to walk around him, quickening my pace, but I should have known he wasn't going to let me go.

His hand shot out, gripping my arm, and twisting me so I was forced to face him once again. "I highly doubt it."

Heat pooled on my skin where his hand held me. "You think you know me? Please." I jerked away, dislodging his hand, but not because I was stronger, or had caught him off guard. He had released me.

"Your name," he insisted.

Geez. If it got him off my back, so be it. "Olivia Campbell," I answered in an even tone, resigned to my fate. If he had been following me for the wallet, why hadn't he mentioned it yet?

"Olivia," he repeated as if testing the sound of my name on his lips. "Now, that wasn't so hard."

Smartass.

"Happy now?" I snapped, prepared to go on my merry way.

He lifted a single brow. "We're just getting started, Cupcake."

"Don't call me that. I gave you my name, even though you haven't given me yours." Did I even want to know? He would probably give me a fake anyway. Damn. Why hadn't I thought of that? I shouldn't have given him my real name. That was so stupid of me. If I was going to survive, I had to be smarter than that.

His lips curved. "It seems we got off on the wrong foot. I'm Jase Dior."

I rubbed my arm not because it hurt, but just the opposite. Tingles radiated from where he'd touched me, confusing me. Jase, huh? He even had a sexy name. Not surprising though, it suited him. I shoved my hands into my back pockets, ignoring the strange sensation. "Why are you so interested in me?" I asked.

He blinked. "I haven't figured it out yet."

A snorting sound came from the back of my throat. "Can you at least tell me why have you been following me?"

"I have a weakness for pretty things."

"Like diamonds? Cars? The sunset?" I asked.

"No, blondes," he replied matter-of-factly.

I choked. An awkward silence descended, and I was still trying to come up with a better plan than my first to get myself out of this situation. I still didn't know what kind of situation I was in. Good? Or bad? "I'm not a natural blonde," I finally said, breaking the silence. It was a lie, but he didn't need to know that.

He crossed his arms, his muscles stretching the fabric of his suit jacket as they covered the taut chest hidden under his shirt. "I can be flexible."

Hell no.

"How old are you?" he asked.

Next, he was going to want to know my bra size, or my social security number. Either way, I wasn't dishing. "Does it matter?"

"No, not really," he admitted, angling his head to the side as he regarded me with those piercing eyes.

What the hell was he getting at? I definitely didn't trust him. Flipping the hood of my sweatshirt over my head, I covered my tousled hair. "You're really starting to weird me out. I'm not interested in any little sex rings you've got going on the side. So it was nice meeting you, Jase." *Hope I never see you again.*

Even as the thought left my mind, I knew it wasn't true. As much as I needed a ridiculous amount of therapy, I couldn't pretend there wasn't something about Jase that captivated me.

"Not so fast." A breeze blew down the alley, carrying his scent in the air. It reminded me of sea spray and moonlight, like a midnight beach party. "You don't belong on the streets."

I snorted. "Thanks for the unnecessary concern, but I do just fine on my own."

He moved forward, so that his warm breath danced along my cheek, and I flinched. "I'm not going to hurt you. It isn't my style to intimidate women," he admitted, shooting me a disarming smile.

He shouldn't be equipped with such a powerful weapon. For a moment, I forgot we stood in the street. That it was freezing outside. That I must look atrocious. The way he stared at me made me not feel alone for the first time in weeks.

"Okay, what is it you want from me? Am I a welfare project? Because I'm not interested in being your charity case."

He forked a hand through his dark hair. "Do you always jump to so many conclusions? I should just pick another girl, but I can't figure out why I'm drawn to you."

"It's the hair, isn't it?" I questioned, remembering his comment about blondes.

His lips might have twitched, but it was hard to tell in the night. "It definitely helps, Cupcake. I need you to come with me."

My brows pulled together. "And if I refuse?"

"It would be easier if you didn't."

My fear was now off the charts. I didn't care how perfect his face was. "Easier for who?"

His gaze locked on mine. "I won't hurt you. I give you my word."

"Sorry, but I don't trust you, and for your word to mean anything, I would have to trust you. So, you see, I think we find ourselves at an impasse." My eyes darted behind him. There was a very slim chance I could take him by surprise and run off. A knee to the groin usually worked, and would give me the window I needed to escape.

"Don't even try it. I will catch you," he warned me, his eyes darkening to a deep plum.

"If you don't let me go, I'll scream."

The stranger's jaw tightened. "Time is running out. We must go."

"I'm not going anywhere with you. No matter how cute your dimples are." I squeezed my eyes shut for a moment. Why did stuff like that always have to come out of my mouth? I needed to learn how to not blurt out the first thing that popped into my head.

He blew out a breath. "I figured you'd want to do this the hard way."

I was about to take my chances and give my lungs some more exercise, when he blew in my face. A cool mist that smelled of lavender and vanilla, and felt like the spray of a waterfall rained over me. I gasped—the worst possible reaction I could have had—inhaling a huge gulp of the mysterious mist. The effect was instant. A heavy calmness overcame me, making my eyes droop.

It took away my fear. It took away everything.

A shriek tore through the darkness, like a soul being tortured. My last thought was I might never get to tell Staci about the hottie I ran into in an alley. She would have loved every second of my discomfort.

I blinked several times, hoping to recognize my location. No such luck. This wasn't the first time I'd woken up in a strange place. However, it was the first time I'd woken up with my wrists tied together.

What the hell?

Thickly corded ropes bound my hands, and no matter how much I tugged, I couldn't loosen the knot. *Breathe, Olivia. You can figure a way out of this. Just Breathe.*

My body quivered, and a veil of panic came over me as my eyes followed my bindings to where the rope attached to a wall. I felt chilled, but unlike the cold I was used to in Chicago, this emanated from the inside.

Where am I?

How did I get here?

Jase! my mind hissed—the hot guy with the dimples who had cornered me in the alley. His face was the last memory I had before my mind went fuzzy. What had he done to me? I should have listened to the stupid voice in my head, the one that had told me to run when I'd had the chance. Now look what I'd gotten myself into—tied to a wall.

At least my clothes were still on.

But for how long? that little voice asked.

Shut up.

"Hello?" I called, my voice echoing through the silent room. "Is anyone there?"

The only sounds were my heavy breathing, and the pounding of my heart. My frantic eyes took in my surroundings: a plush bed in the corner, soft cream carpet on the floor, and flickering candles casting a soft glow.

At least I wasn't in a dungeon or a cellar. I had that going for me.

Opening my mouth, I was about to call out again—louder this time—when the clopping of footsteps approached outside the door. The knob turned, and I shifted straighter in the chair, prepared to fight if necessary.

But that implied I knew how to fight, and I didn't.

Four extraordinary guys strolled in, their eyes immediately finding me in the room. One I might have been able to handle, but four? How the hell could I take on four? They gathered around me in a semicircle. I had to crane my neck to look at them since they were all tall, built like football players, and extremely good looking. I had thought Jase had muddled my brain, but four of them? All coherent thoughts went out the window. Each was different in his coloring and look, but they all held a sense of power and importance.

Jase stood in the middle. At least I knew who to blame for my capture. To his left was a guy who looked as if he belonged in a punk rock band. His hair was spiked down the center and green-tipped. His emerald eyes twinkled when he noticed me staring at the metal ring in his bottom lip. He winked, letting me know he noticed I was checking him out.

On the other side of Jase stood a golden god—olive skin, whiskey-colored eyes tinged with crimson, caramel brown hair, and full beautiful lips. Beside him was the fourth. Whereas the others seemed approachable, the blond with icy blue eyes was the fiercest of the four, and also the biggest. His lips formed a thin line as he eyed me with disdain. He reminded me of an ice prince.

"Welcome to the Veil Isles, Olivia," Jase greeted, in that calm and sensual voice.

"She is quite beautiful," the one with the mohawk and hot lips added.

Golden God smirked. "Did you expect anything less from Jase? She fits his type to a T." His voice was like honey, thick and sweet.

"You better be right about her," the blond replied in a sharp tone.

"Trust me, this one is different, Issik," Jase assured him.

"So you said the last one hundred and ninety-nine times," Golden God muttered.

They had done this one hundred and ninety-nine times? Kidnapping girls? My eyes went wide with fear. What kind of crap did I get myself into?

"Don't look so alarmed. Who knows? Maybe Jase is right," Hot Lips said, rewarding me with a wicked grin. "You could be the one we've been searching for."

I didn't really care if I was the *one*. In all honesty, I hoped I wasn't so I could get as far away from these four as possible… and this place called the Veil Isles. "Can you untie me now?"

Jase lifted a dark brow. "Depends. Are you going to run? Because I'm not in the mood to chase you through the castle."

Castle, my mind echoed.

"He might not be, but I am." Hot Lips winked.

"Kieran," Jase scolded. "Do we have your word, Cupcake?"

The three guys on either side of Jase smirked, even the cold one, Issik, his lips twitching.

"Fine," I agreed, while cursing the four of them under my breath. "But call me cupcake one more time, and I'll be forced to introduce my knee to your junk."

A few snickers erupted as Jase bent down and fumbled with the knot, loosening it so he could slip it over my hands. "Better?" Now he suddenly cared about my well-being.

Rubbing my hands over my wrists, I tried to release some

25

of the sting from the bonds. "Are you going to tell me what I'm doing here? What is the Veil? And why did you kidnap me?" I presumed it was because I had been living on the streets, and Jase knew no one would be looking for me.

He had assumed correctly, but I wouldn't admit it.

"You have questions, clearly," Jase added, sounding too calm and collected for someone who had just committed abduction.

Duh. I think I had made that point already. "Did you think I wouldn't?"

Issik scowled.

Kieran smirked.

Jase frowned.

And the golden god, whose name I still didn't know, coughed.

"I like her," Kieran said. "Can we keep her?"

Ice Prince's jaw tightened. He was every inch the image of a Viking. "It doesn't really matter if you do or don't like her. She is here for a reason. Don't forget that."

"And just what the hell is that reason?" I demanded.

"It's complicated," Jase answered. "I think we should get you settled in, let you clean up, and rest. Tomorrow will be soon enough to answer those questions I see swimming in your eyes. And before you argue, remember, there are four of us."

They all loomed over me, daring me to challenge them with their stern demeanors and firm abs. Damn the four of them to the deepest parts of hell. "It doesn't look like I have much of a choice in the matter."

Jase hovered over me, power exuding from his chest. "You have no reason to trust me, but I saved you. You no longer have to live on the streets or steal to eat. You don't have to worry about where you're going to sleep. Do us all a favor and don't do anything foolish."

I tipped my chin up, feeling my cheeks flood with color. He might not have meant to embarrass me on purpose, but he did so all the same. My pride refused to admit that what he offered sounded like an answer to my prayers. Too good to be true.

I was struck again by his handsomeness, but it didn't last more than a few seconds before my sanity returned. Me? Do something foolish? A glint in his expression gave me pause, and I couldn't determine why I wasn't demanding him to let me go, or why I wasn't threatening him. "What happens if I decide I don't want to stay? Am I allowed to leave, or are you going to stop me?"

The four of them suddenly couldn't look me in the eye, and I knew I had my answer. They weren't going to let me go. After a minute, Jase took a deep breath. "I give you my word no harm will come to you. You'll be under my protection."

"Protection from what? Am I in danger?"

Kieran crossed his arms and gave me a cheeky smile. "This one is a lot quicker and calmer than the others. We're keeping her."

"She's not nearly as frightened as she should be," Ice Prince added, his frown deepening.

Oh, there was a good dose of fear inside me. I was just better at faking it. I took a second to study Issik. He oozed bitterness—a warrior with a chip on his shoulder. His silky blond hair hung straight, just reaching his chin, which was covered with day-old stubble. It suited him.

"Don't let her doe-eyed face fool you, Zade. She's scared."

I wanted to wipe the smugness off Jase's pretty face after his words. Bastard. I was starting to really not like him, but at least I had gotten the last one's name—Zade, the one who looked like a golden god.

27

"Will the four of you stop talking about me as if I wasn't in the room?" I shouted.

That got their attention.

"This will be interesting for sure. Do you think she'll get along with the others?" Kieran asked.

Jase was no longer amused, the pupils of his violet eyes sobering. "We're keeping her separate until we know for sure if she can be the one."

Zade lifted a cinnamon brow. "Is that the only reason?"

I opened my mouth to complain yet again, but Issik beat me to it. "How old are you?" he asked, directing the question to me.

Under his piercing eyes, I fidgeted in the chair. "Why does it matter? If you have no qualms about kidnapping, I doubt my age is suddenly going to give you a conscience."

There were a few snickers.

Jase shook his head. "This room will be yours for the time being."

My gaze swung to the door. "Let me guess, there's a lock."

"You got it, Cupcake, not that it matters. There's no leaving the Veil Isles."

We'll see about that. If there was a will, there was a way. "I thought I told you not to call me that."

"Try not to—" Jase was interrupted by a loud shriek.

All four glorious heads swung to the balcony doors I had failed to notice in the room before.

What was that? It sounded like a bear being tortured. Their hard bodies stiffened as each of the guys' faces became dark scowls. A large shadow flew over the window, causing the room to go black for a moment as it moved past. It was a lot bigger than your average hawk or crow.

Sweet Jesus.

"Dammit," Jase growled, causing trepidation to dance inside my chest.

"What is it?" I asked, my eyes bouncing between the four of them. Each guy was glowering, so I could only conclude it wasn't good.

"A wraith," Issik hissed, swinging his frozen glare to Jase. "Did you forget to close the portal?"

"No, of course not," he replied. "I'm not an idiot."

Issik lips thinned as he strutted to the double doors that led outside. "How did it get through, then?"

Another scream echoed, both long and piercing. I didn't know what a wraith was, but I also didn't want to know. My mind was kind of still hung up on the word "portal." That couldn't mean what I thought it did, could it? No. It wasn't possible. Traveling from one place to another through a swirling black hole?

Jase sighed. "I've got it. Stay with her," he told Hot Lips and Golden God, walking toward the French doors. I caught a flash of something on his face before he spun away, and if I already weren't having the most otherworldly day, I would have brushed off the speck of worry I thought I glimpsed.

Angling my head so I could see around the bulky form of

Issik, my eyes bulged. Jase tossed his cotton shirt over his head, revealing chiseled abs. *I won't lie, for a moment, my mind went blank and my mouth dry.* I stretched to the side for a better view, but the bellow of another roar outside snapped me back.

The wraith, as they called it, was clearly pissed off. I didn't know what Jase thought he could do about it. I knew what I wanted to do: curl up in the corner and cry. This day was taking its toll.

But my emotions were pushed aside as I stared at Jase, my mind rejecting everything it was seeing. Dark purple scales that were almost black appeared on his shoulders, multiplying until they covered his entire torso. His fingers went to the button on his pants and off those went too.

Um, this was way more than I'd bargained for. His violet eyes brightened as the transformation took over.

I bit my lip to keep from screaming, because some inner voice told me that was not the right response, and would only make this situation worse. Three other pairs of eyes all watched me with intensity, judging my reaction.

Claws exploded from his fingertips and toes. He was already a tall and muscular guy, but his body grew, filling out and lengthening. Scales covered his entire form. A massive tail unraveled from behind him and across the room from one wall to the other.

My eyes swept the length of him from head to tail. What Jase had changed into, nearly made me pee my pants. He was a mother-freaking dragon.

I held back a squeak as he angled his triangular head toward me, and if it weren't for those violet eyes, I wouldn't have believed it was possible. I felt positive this creature could do a serious amount of damage; his sheer height and powerful tail were formidable enough on their own. Then he took off, spreading his massive wings when he leaped off the balcony.

"I'm not letting him have all the fun," Kieran announced, whipping off his shirt.

Oh my god. Please tell me they aren't all going to get naked and shift into dragons. I didn't think my nerves could handle it.

Dragons! my mind screamed. I'd been abducted by a group of sexy dragons. Or at least two of them...

It wasn't possible, but I had just seen it with my own eyes.

Kieran walked across the room, and in a similar fashion, his body changed and stretched, but his scales were green with long spikes lining the end of his tail. Dipping his head, he followed Jase into the dark sky.

My heart hammered in my chest, and I expected, any second, it was going to jump out. This kind of stuff didn't happen to me. It only existed in movies and fantasy novels. Had they injected me with drugs today? What the hell had been in that pizza? Was I dreaming? That had to be it. This was a nightmare, and I would wake up at any moment alone in my little shack behind the food mart.

I squeezed my eyes closed, praying when I opened them that all this would disappear.

Crap.

Issik and Zade stared down at me with twin expressions of curiosity.

Dammit.

"She hasn't freaked out yet," Zade said to Issik, possibly impressed with my composure. If he only knew what was going on inside me.

Issik's lips pressed together firmly. "I wouldn't be so sure about that. She's probably in shock."

I shoved off the chair, not caring if they tried to stop me. I had to see what was happening with my own two eyes. Were there really two dragons flying around outside this castle? Was I really in a castle at all?

Neither objected when I stood, but they followed me outside to stand on the balcony. I gasped. The view was... breathtaking. I'd never seen anything like it in my life. I had to be at least six stories high, and directly below me was a body of water that surrounded the entire castle, almost as if we were in a stranded oasis. Beyond the flowing sea were dark trees of various heights, and further yet, I could just make out through the fog three other castles with multiple towers that jutted into the sky and disappeared into black clouds.

"What do you think of your first glimpse of the Veil Isles?" Zade asked, leaning so he could whisper in my ear.

A shudder rippled through my body, and I couldn't tell if it was because of his proximity or the shock, but I was rendered speechless. My hands gripped the edge of the balcony's railing as I searched the sky and found what I was looking for. Proof my eyes hadn't deceived me. The two dragons soaring in the night were easy to spot; their impressive wings spread wide as they glided in the air, circling a small figure. "Small" was only a relative term to the size of the dragons, because next to me, this dark creature would have dwarfed me.

The shadowy figure moved with a deathly grace that filled my veins with ice. Then again, Issik had moved closer. He could very well have been responsible for the sudden coldness running through my blood.

I didn't know which I should be scared of more: the dragons or the wraith. Or the two guys flanking me.

I thought the night would have made it hard to discern between the dragons, but I spotted Jase easily enough. His scales glistened in the moonlight, and it was difficult to believe only moments ago he'd been standing in front of me.

The breath in my lungs escaped as my eyes followed his movements. Jase and Kieran seemed to work together, taking turns swinging their claws at the wraith while they hovered in the air supported by their wings. I could hear the flapping as their wings beat, both powerful and elegant.

The wraith fought with precision and ruthfullness. With twice the speed of the dragons, it weaved between Kieran and Jase. Kieran opened his jaws, letting a stream of neon green fire expel from within him, straight at the wraith. The creature let out another bellowing shriek, but didn't run away. In fact, just the opposite. He apparently did not fear the dragons.

Me?

I was afraid of everything at the moment.

But even with the huge amounts of fear swimming inside me, I couldn't tear my gaze from the action. It was like the most engrossing movie of my life, but instead of watching from the comforts of a recliner with a bowl of popcorn, I was an active participant. Everything I thought I knew about dragons—which, to be frank, was all from fiction anyway—seemed to be wrong. What happened to dragons spitting red fire? Kieran's dragon breath was so much cooler.

If I thought I'd had questions before, it was nothing compared to the absurd number racing wildly in my head now.

Jase and Kieran kept a tight leash on the wraith, following it as the beast flew just under the balcony. A gust of wind blew my hair back as the trio rushed through the air. I leaned over the railing, stretching to see them, and the next thing I knew, I was tumbling, falling through the darkness toward the black sea below.

My scream rang out over the valley.

The dark waters were rushing quickly toward me, and I braced myself. *Oh God, I'm going to die.* That was really going to piss Jase off. He went to all the trouble of getting me here —for reasons I still didn't understand—and then I go and get myself killed. Classic Olivia.

But I didn't smack the murky sea as I'd expected. I landed on something firm and scaly when it swept underneath me, catching me before I cannonballed. As the air was forced from my lungs on impact, my hands fumbled to grasp something for fear of falling again. Clinging to the dragon's scales around his neck, I tried to catch my breath. Wind tore at my face, and I buried my head deeper against his neck.

I wasn't sure which dragon had rescued me, but if I had to guess, it was Issik, the ice prince, since the shimmering scales underneath me were a whitish-blue. Although the scales were not as rough as I would have thought. We were still diving downward at frightening speeds toward the water, but at the last second, he pulled up, letting his hind legs and tail skim over the surface.

"You're intentionally trying to scare the shit out of me, aren't you?" I yelled, when my heart started beating again.

"Are you always this suicidal?" Issik's voice sounded in my head, proving I had been right about which dragon had saved me.

"Depends if I'm having a good day or not. And let me tell you, today has sucked the big one," I muttered.

"Think you can manage to hang on, while I get you somewhere you can't get hurt?"

My legs tightened around him as if I was born to ride dragons. Just like riding a bike, I told myself. "As long as you don't do any loop the loops."

I swore I felt his body rumble in a laugh.

Holy crap. I was riding a dragon.

Now that I was safe, for the time being, I could see more of the land. I had been wrong about the castle being surrounded entirely by water. On the other side, black sand covered the ground, leading to a gigantic volcano. Billows of smoke rose from the top, dissolving into the black clouds. It was evident I wasn't in Chicago anymore. The land here was lush and vibrant, yet somber. Regardless of its beauty, it emitted danger.

The dragons flying around were proof enough of that.

Above us, Jase, Kieran, and the wraith came into sight. The shrouded creature screeched in rage. Jase thrashed his thick tail through the air, smacking the wraith and sending him spiraling straight at Issik and me.

"Hang on tight," Issik advised me as he reared back.

My arms wrapped around his neck, gripping on for dear life.

Issik inhaled deeply, and my mind screamed in warning. What goes in must come out. He blew an icy mist directly into the creature's face, a second before it sunk razor-sharp choppers into the dragon's scaly flesh.

A whimpering noise came from the back of Issik's throat, but he held steadfast, never wavering regardless that he was hurt.

The wraith's ethereal body crystallized, turning into an ice sculpture. Kieran flew down, whacking the spiked end of his tail into the wraith, and shattering it like glass. The pieces rained down into the murky waters below.

That was the single scariest and coolest shit that had ever happened to me.

Threat averted, Issik flew us back to the balcony with Jase and Kieran close behind. *"You think you can manage to get down without hurting yourself?"* Issik asked with a bitter sharpness.

Out of the four guys, Issik was the hardest to read. He didn't really seem to like me all that much; yet, he was the one who had saved me. "As long as you stay still for a minute," I retorted, swinging both my legs to one side.

He tipped his head, and I slid down his neck. Zade was there to catch me. Once my feet were safely on the ground, I spun around to get my first full look at Issik in his dragon form. He was utterly stunning. At the end of his enormous white wings, where they sloped into waves, were talons. His icy blue eyes glowed brightly as they pinned mine. Everything about him reminded me of Chicago winters—cold, blistering, ruthless.

Jase and Kieran had already shifted back and stood outside the bedroom door fully dressed, watching me as I gawked at Issik. In a reverse transformation, the dragon shifted into a man, who became a naked Issik. He raised a brow as I continued to gape, my gaze wandering over him. Who could blame me? He was an incredible male specimen. It was like a shield came down over Issik—his brief flicker of amusement washed away by the hardness now reflected in his eyes as he slipped into his discarded clothes.

After all the excitement, the moment finally caught up to me. I huddled in the corner, my body wracked with violent shivers. I was a pretty open-minded individual, but this... this was way outside my scope of reality.

Four sets of eyes stared at me as if I might shatter into a million pieces at any moment. Questions spun like a windmill through my head. How in the world did they turn into dragons? Did it hurt? Could it be an illusion? Were they aliens from another planet? Or maybe a science experiment with dinosaur DNA?—Jurassic Park came to mind. And if there were dragon... er, shifters... then why not a wraith? But most importantly, why did it attack us?

If I could only get those thoughts to form into words... but my mouth was numb. Placing a hand on the nearest wall, I leaned my hip against it.

"So, how was she?" Kieran asked Issik, bumping his shoulder lightly against the ice prince's.

Issik frowned. "Wouldn't you like to know."

Not getting what he wanted from Issik, Kieran turned to me. "How was your first time, Olivia?" The way he asked that had my cheeks flaming. Something about how Hot Lips worded things and his playful tone gave off a sexy vibe.

I ignored him and finally found my tongue. "W-what just happened?" I stammered.

"It's pretty common, actually," Kieran answered, a lazy grin on his lips. It was evident he loved the thrill of the hunt, of flying, and of being a dragon.

"Which part? That thing that attacked us, or you turning into dragons?" I needed specifics.

"The wraith was a messenger," Jase supplied.

"A messenger?" I echoed on the verge of hysteria. "I'm guessing it wasn't a friendly message."

The four of them shared a look, and seemed to be deciding how much to tell me before Jase turned to face me with an expression of incredulity. "You're scared... but not because I turned into a dragon?"

Truth be told, I was terrified, but yes, I was way more scared of the other thing. The wraith had an aura about it akin to death. As weird as this was, at least they had turned back into humans. I couldn't say the same about the other creature. That had to count for something. "I would be lying if I said I wasn't scared. Nothing about what I've just witnessed seems real, and I keep waiting to wake up, but on the off chance this is not a dream, I'm also... curious, I guess. Do all four of you turn into dragons?"

"Pretty fucking awesome, right?" Kieran said, grinning like the shithead I felt positive he was. The others didn't bat an eye.

"And you each breathe a different kind of fire or... some-thing?" I questioned, processing the assumptions tumbling in my head. I was trying to make sense of it all, but I probably sounded like an idiot in the process.

With slow movements, Jase walked toward me. "It's been a long night, Cupcake. Why don't you get some sleep? In the morning, we'll explain everything. I think you've had enough excitement. I don't want to push you too fast."

"This can't be real," I muttered to myself, laying a hand on my forehead.

"I know this might all seem impossible, but get some rest. You'll see things clearer after you've slept." Jase kept his voice smooth and level.

Will I though?

Would I wake up in the abandoned building behind the Quick Mart—alone once again? Could this all be a dream?

Something told me a good night's sleep wasn't going to make it all better.

Jase flashed me a set of dimples, capturing my eyes with his, so that the other three guys melted away. There was something mesmerizing and magnetic about Jase. "Rest, Cupcake," he whispered, and for the second time tonight, he blew a puff of purple mist into my face.

"Why do you keep doing that?" I mumbled, my eyes growing sleepy, and I knew I only had a few more moments before I wouldn't be able to stand on my own, but it turned out, that wasn't a problem.

Jase bent down, swooping an arm under my legs and lifting me up. I rested my heavy head on his shoulders, unable to support it myself. My face pressed up against his neck, and I inhaled the scent of him—sand and sea. "Because your body needs to sleep, and you strike me as the kind of girl who is stubborn. I'm giving you what you need. Now, close your eyes," he demanded, walking me into the center of the room.

So much for insisting on getting answers. Jase had even taken that from me. Now I had no choice but to sleep.

Just who are they?

What do they want with me?

Damn. Damn. Damn.

I lost the battle with consciousness before he laid me down.

Snuggling deeper into the warmth surrounding me, I kept my eyes closed, telling myself to go back to sleep, to ignore the blissful sun glowing on my cheeks. I didn't want to stir, for that meant I would have to face the reality that my life had become a fantasy, and not in a good way. It was so much easier to keep dreaming and pretend I wouldn't wake to a nightmare.

Maybe if I wished hard enough, I would be back home in my own bed. Mom would be downstairs humming, and life would go back to normal.

It was such a nice dream.

A firm knock sounded on the door, and I threw the covers over my head, wishing he would go away. A frown pulled at my lips. I was miffed about having my sleep disturbed. The door creaked open, and I held my breath, staying as still as possible under the covers.

"You going to sleep all day?" a husky voice asked. "I thought you would be brimming with questions this morning." It was Kieran. The rocker embodying a dragon had the tiniest hint of an accent.

"Go away," I groaned, my voice muffled under the thick blanket.

Kieran laughed, and the sound made my belly cartwheel.

My scowl deepened. *Stop that,* I berated my body. *You should feel nothing but contempt for him... for all four of them.*

Light fingers tugged on the end of the covers, pulling them down so I stared up into Kieran's twinkling emerald eyes. His piercing glittered in the sun, and I wondered what it would be like to kiss someone with a lip ring. Would the metal be cool against my mouth? Would I be tempted to bite it?

I shook my head.

Why are you thinking about kissing him? He is holding you hostage, remember?

"I brought you something to eat," he offered.

My gaze was drawn to a small table where a tray sat, the smells wafting around the room. "Where's Jase?" I asked, giving up the pretense of sleep. I was wide awake now, and my stomach was growling.

Kieran lifted a brow. "Would you prefer him over me?"

He was impossible. I shrugged because I was sure his ego would take a hit. "It doesn't really matter. Am I still a prisoner?"

The mattress dipped to the side with his weight as he sat on the edge of the bed. "I like to think of it as a guest."

Linking my fingers together, I stared up at him. "You have a warped sense of hospitality."

"If you give it a chance, I think you'll enjoy living in the Veil Isles. Believe it or not, we aren't monsters."

"Right, because the wraith was so warm and welcoming."

His lips twitched. "They are pesky bastards. Eat. And then I'll take you to clean up."

A shower. My mind sighed. Warm food, a clean bed, a hot bath—were they trying to butter me up?

I plucked a piece of toast off the tray and had it to my mouth before I paused. "How do I know this isn't poisoned?"

Kieran grabbed the other half of the toast and bit into it. "Happy?" he asked, swallowing. "I don't normally poison pretty girls," he added with a wink.

I took a nibble from the corner, refraining from gorging myself by shoving the whole piece in my mouth. I studied him as I ate, thinking about what he'd said. "Is that your ability? Poison?"

A gleam of surprise leapt into his eyes. "You're perceptive. Maybe too much. Yes, I breathe poison; it's my curse."

I thought it odd he considered being a dragon-shifter a curse. "Issik breathes ice. Jase some kind of sleeping spell?" I guessed, listing off their abilities.

"Tranquility," he supplied.

"What about Zade?" I asked.

"Fire," he replied.

After polishing off the toast, I moved on to a cup of fruit —none of which I recognized. Still, my hunger at this point wasn't picky. "Where are the others?"

Kieran shrugged and seemed content just keeping me company. "Around. We each have our own kingdoms to oversee. This is Jase's, Wakeland Kingdom, and his castle, Wakeland Keep."

"So you all don't live here?"

Kieran shook his head. "But don't worry, blondie, you'll get to see plenty of me."

Again, his tone implied something wicked.

I scooted to the other side of the bed and stood up, stretching my legs. I had slept in my clothes last night, and was glad to see no one had tried to remove them. With my hunger now curbed, I thought about the mention of a shower.

"Come on. I'll show you to the bath house," Kieran

offered, as I ran my fingers through my hair.

It was hopeless. Nothing but a bottle of deep conditioner and a brush would fix this mess.

Exiting the chamber, Kieran led us down a long passageway. The walls were made of dark gray limestone, and our footsteps echoed off the wood floors. The corridors were lit by torches hung in sconces. We turned a corner and descended a set of winding stairs. Inside, I couldn't figure out how to feel. Scared? Fascinated? Foolish? Should I be trying to escape?

There were no railings as we walked down the steps, and me being me, I stumbled, by not looking ahead, and spending too much time admiring the paintings lining the walls. My nails scrambled against the rock as I tried to catch myself from plummeting, but really, I had little to worry about.

Kieran's quick reflexes saved me, his hands landing on my waist. "You're going to be quite the challenge to keep safe, aren't you?" he whispered as he pulled me up against him to steady us both.

"Huh?" I uttered, my brain fuzzy. *What did he say?* It didn't really seem to matter. My eyes couldn't get past his lips.

His chest rumbled against mine. "Curious?" he asked, running the pad of his thumb along the side of my jaw, skimming just under my lower lip. His head dipped, and my lashes began to flutter closed. He was going to kiss me.

"Kieran!" snapped a cold voice.

Hot Lips kissed the tip of my nose instead, grinning down at my wide eyes. "Issik takes the fun out of everything."

My eyes glanced over Kieran's shoulder to see the tall blond stalking toward us with purposeful strides. I jumped out of the punk rocker's arms, standing on my own without his support, and immediately missing the strength of his body.

What the hell is wrong with me?

Kieran shot a lopsided grin at Issik as he started to walk again. "Relax, mate. Olivia and I were just getting to know each other better. Isn't that right, blondie?"

Issik wasn't buying it. "Get her cleaned up. Don't play with her."

I winced. *Asshole*.

I bit my tongue to keep from saying something that would anger him further. Issik didn't strike me as the type of guy who put up with nonsense. Kieran slipped a hand to the small of my back, urging me, with a slight pressure, to keep moving. I was all too happy to oblige. Issik gave me the chills.

The castle was bigger than I imagined. Left on my own, there was no way I would be able to find my way back to my room. We had to be close to the first floor when Kieran pushed through a set of doors, a wave of heat hitting me. Inside was a large room with ivory pillars that stretched to the vaulted ceilings. At the center of the space, steam pillowed over a square pool, much like a hot tub. It was open and big enough for six people.

The bath house was a public facility. Talk about medieval.

I spun on Kieran. "You guys don't believe in privacy?"

"You're not shy, are you?"

I shifted my feet, unwilling to admit any of my faults to someone who might use them against me. "I never said that."

His lips curved. "Once we're sure you've adjusted, you'll be free to wander at your will. Until then, one of us will be at your side at all times."

"Joy," I mumbled.

I moved behind one of the elaborate columns, slipping off my grimy shoes and socks. Kieran guarded the door, leaning against the wall, but from where I stood, he couldn't really see me. The shifter chuckled, knowing I hid from his eyes.

The heat in my cheeks heightened as I whipped off my hoodie and shirt, leaving me standing in my bra and jeans.

My fingers fumbled with the buttons. I wanted to hurry up and get under the cover of the steaming, bubbly water. Slipping the rest of my clothes off, I stepped onto the first landing, the hot water floating over my toes. Closing my eyes and sighing, I took the next two steps in a rush. My foot slipped, and I belly flopped into the pool. Water rushed over my head.

That was one way to get clean.

I came up, sputtering and snorting, my drenched hair hanging over my face. Shoving the mass of blonde strands out of my eyes, I groaned. Kieran was crouched at the edge of the bath, shaking his head and smirking. "You gave me a fright. For a second, I thought you were drowning yourself."

My lips seemed to be in a permanent frown ever since I got here. "I'm fine," I assured him through my teeth.

"Jase really outdid himself this time," Kieran added, as he walked back to guard the doorway.

I exhaled. His hovering made me self-conscious.

Along the side of the marble tub sat a tray of soaps, oils, and lotions that would have made Bath & Body Works jealous. The bottles and bars didn't have labels, so I just plucked one up and began working it into my hair. As the soap foamed, the room was scented like coconut shells. The warmth and the exotic fragrance made me feel as if I was bathing in a Hawaiian waterfall.

I had just finished dunking my head underwater, rinsing the bubbles out of my hair, when a girl sauntered in. She had long golden brown locks, and lush red lips that made her creamy skin appear flawless. Without so much as batting an eye, she dropped the silk robe she wore, and like a swan, gracefully lowered herself into the bath.

I stayed as still as a statue, not pleased at having my privacy invaded, but at the same time, it was nice to see another face that wasn't male.

She eyed me warily. "So you're the new shade of blonde?" I detected traces of envy in her voice.

Her? Jealous of me? Was she insane? All she had to do was look in the mirror.

"I guess?" I replied, unsure how to answer. My hair was blonde, so…

She skimmed a slender hand over the top of the water. "I'm Harlow."

"Olivia."

"A bit of friendly advice, *Olivia*. I might not be the chosen one, but this is *my* house." The implication came through loud and clear. She didn't want me stepping on her territory. Nothing was welcoming about Harlow.

"Trust me, you have nothing to worry about."

Harlow shot hazel daggers at me. "That's what we all said."

I frowned. "How many are there?"

She chuckled, and not in an approachable way. "Here in Jase's kingdom? I've lost count."

As long as she was willing to answer, I was going to pepper her with questions. Pressing my back against the wall, I kept to my side of the bath. "Why are we here?"

"They haven't told you yet?" Hatred dripped off her lips while she dunked deeper into the water, resting her head back. I shook my head. "It isn't my place to tell you. Besides, from the looks of you, there is no way you can be the one they are looking for." Every word out of her mouth was meant to make me feel insignificant and naïve.

I'd had enough. It wasn't my choice to be here. "What the hell is wrong with me?" I shot back. Thinking Harlow and I weren't going to be friends, I let my irritation mask my disappointment. Hopefully, the other girls weren't all as "*friendly*" as the viper Harlow.

She sneered, standing up and letting beads of water run

down her perfect frame—not a shy bone in her body. "It doesn't matter what I think. Just remember your place." Then she stooped down to pick up her discarded robe and walked off.

And what place was that?

"Later, Kieran," I heard her say in a husky voice before the door opened.

It was becoming clear that I had no allies, no one I could trust here in the Veil. I only had myself to rely on. At least that was not much different than my life in Chicago.

"Let's go," Kieran urged, interrupting my perfect dream of lying on the beach, and soaking up the sun as the water lapped at my feet. "The others are waiting for us." He held out a giant towel, stretching from one hand to the other.

My skin was as wrinkly as a raisin, but I couldn't have cared less. Since Harlow's disturbing visit, I'd been trying not to dwell on what little information I had discovered. I stared up at Kieran, crossing my arms over my chest. "Am I expected to go naked?"

His mouth tipped up into a one-sided smile. "I wouldn't object, but I'm guessing you would. There is a closet of clothes just through those doors. Pick anything you would like."

"Close your eyes," I commanded.

The smirk on his lips deepened, but he did as I asked. Water splashed as I rose out of the bathing pool, quickly taking the towel and wrapping it around my body. I held it closed with one hand and squeezed the water from my hair with the other. Kieran opened his eyes, capturing me with his. I hadn't noticed that his hands had moved to my hips until his fingers pressed lightly, drawing my gaze downward.

"You can release me," I said softly.

The center of his bright eyes twinkled. "Promise you're not going to fall and break your neck?"

I rolled my eyes. "Do you want me to lie?"

He only shook his head.

Keeping the towel secured around me, I padded around a white column to the doors Kieran had indicated. They slid open to reveal a small room, filled with everything from dresses to undergarments. *Why do they have so many women's clothes?* I tried not to let it freak me out, but it was pointless. My breathing quickened as I scanned the apparel. *Where are the yoga pants and T-shirts?* My hand ran over the sheer fabric of what I thought was a dress, but it seemed to be missing some key parts. He didn't actually expect me to wear this, right?

I grabbed the first thing my hand touched, resolving myself to look like a harlot because, obviously, that was what they were into here. Trying to figure out how to get it on was a joke, and I absolutely refused to ask the dragon for help— eventually I managed.

The soft seafoam material draped over my body in a Greek goddess style, leaving my sides exposed.

"Everything okay in there?" Kieran called through the cracked doors.

I bit my lower lip, searching a rack of shoes for something that would fit. Grabbing a pair of slip-ons, I stuck them on my feet and turned to push open the door. "No. Everything is not okay. I'm stuck in a strange land. I've been kidnapped by four hot guys. And I have no clue why."

A smug grin split Kieran's lips, his silver hoop twinkling. "You think I'm hot?"

Shit. Did I say that out loud?

His eyes roamed over my body, adding more color to my already flushed cheeks.

"I'm sure some girls find you good-looking," I grumbled, crossing my arms over myself, but it did nothing to make me feel less exposed.

He gave a little jerk of his head to the side. "Come on. I think it's time you learn what you're really doing here."

Took them long enough.

~

Kieran led me to a room that looked like what I would describe as a den from the Dark Ages. No windows made the room dim; the only source of light came from the flickering hearth. Jase sat behind a wooden desk, leaning lazily in an oversized chair. Issik and Zade were sprawled with their legs out on two chocolate-colored couches. All eyes turned to me as I walked in, and my cheeks brightened under their scrutiny.

They continued to stare at me with something akin to curiosity. *What do they see when they look at me?* I jutted my chin out. *What does it matter what they think? Their opinion isn't important.*

And yet, I stood there, feeling awkward and self-conscious.

"Not half bad after a bath," Kieran offered, grinning as he took a seat beside Zade, which left me the only empty spot in the room—next to Ice Prince.

Issik watched me with cool eyes.

"Are my looks that important?" I snapped, not happy about being put on display for them to ogle. I quickly sat on the far side of the couch, leaving as much space between me and Issik as possible. He shifted, taking up most of the couch, so that our legs almost touched, and he had done it on purpose.

I glared.

"No, it's just unexpected," Jase finally spoke up.

Did he mean that in a good or bad way? "I could say the same about the four of you." I hadn't expected them to turn into dragons. Life was full of surprises.

Kieran laughed. "What Jase is *trying* to say, but bumbling it badly, is you're quite beautiful, Olivia."

The color in my cheeks deepened. "Oh."

"But then again, Jase is known as a collector of pretty things," Zade added.

"Like blondes? I'm not your trophy," I retorted, feeling a flicker of annoyance spark inside me.

Jase scowled at Kieran and Zade, his violet eyes darkening.

"Is someone going to explain why I'm here? Or are we just going to make faces at each other?" I asked dryly.

Jase sighed. "Fair enough. You know we're dragon shifters. Our kind has existed for hundreds of thousands of years. We once lived among humans, fought beside them, until our world—and others' like ours—were split from the human realm."

"What do you mean 'other worlds'?" I interrupted him.

"The Veil Isles isn't the only land to house beings with extraordinary abilities. There are many others hidden from the human world," Zade elaborated.

"Is that where the wraith came from?" I asked.

"Sort of," Kieran replied.

"The Great War drove us to hide our world with portals, or we risked seeing it fall to destruction," Jase continued, leaning forward so his elbows rested on the wooden desk. "Our fathers ruled the kingdoms within the Veil—Iculon, Crimson, Viperus, and Wakeland—and did so for many peaceful years until the uprising."

I had no clue what Great War or uprising they were

talking about. I had learned none of this in school during my history lessons.

"A supernatural war came to our doorstep, spilling the blood of our people, of our families, and our friends. To end the massacre, our fathers enlisted a witch by the name of Tianna, to cast a curse on the portal into the Veil before they were killed, but the witch had an agenda of her own. Her betrayal cost the dragon shifters everything." A muscle along Jase's jaw thumped as he talked about the witch. He definitely harbored some nasty feelings toward her.

As I sat and listened, I tried not to think about Issik's cool leg against mine. His body temperature seemed to be set at freezing all the time.

Kieran clenched his hands into fists, tension lining his body. "Tianna sealed the portal as our fathers planned, but only to their direct lineage. Her treachery trapped us here, and while others could leave, they eventually never returned —either killed or enslaved by the wraiths that guard the portal. And there was nothing we could do about it."

"We've been stranded on this island for nearly a hundred years. Never allowed to age, have families, or escape, except for a single night, twice a year, during the summer and winter solstices. We've spent the last ten decades trying to unweave the spell Tianna cast. We're the last dragons in the world," Jase explained.

A witch?

A dying breed?

A curse?

My mind whirled. This was a heartbreaking and *tragic* story, but I still didn't understand what I had to do with it. "What happens if you don't return after the solstices?" I asked.

All four men stiffened.

"There was a fifth dragon heir: Tobias." Zade spoke up,

after a few tense moments passed. His cinnamon eyes swirled. "He tested that very theory, regardless of the warnings Tianna had issued before she departed from the Veil. We knew it was suicide, but he was foolish, and believed he had enough strength to resist Tianna's hex. His might didn't save him. When he didn't return before sunrise the day after the winter solstice, his body burst into flames as the curse had forewarned, leaving behind only the bones of his dragon skeleton Tianna has taunted us with his death since."

I suppressed a shudder. Being burned alive was no joke. "What does any of this have to do with me?" I asked.

"The curse Tianna cast can only be broken by a girl who holds the key to our freedom," Kieran informed me.

"Are you talking about a tangible key or a metaphorical one?" I didn't have any magical key in my possession. Hell, I had barely anything in my possession. My cell phone was the most expensive thing I owned.

"We don't know," Jase admitted. "Tianna used a blood curse to trap us, and we believe the blood of the chosen will set us free from this prison. We've spent years searching for the one who can break it."

And they thought that person might be me—that was laughable.

I actually started to chuckle, until all four pairs of eyes pinned me with a look of, What in the actual fuck is wrong with her? "You can't possibly think that it's me," I rebutted.

"That's why you're here," Issik said, speaking for the first time. He left no room for questioning. His voice was firm with a bit of that arctic blast coming through.

They were serious.

"The sight of my own blood makes me faint. No, I can't do it." I shook my head.

Issik's piercing eyes were directly on mine. "We're not giving you much choice in the matter."

Well, damn. "And if I'm not the one to break it, I'm stuck here. Is that what you're telling me?"

"It doesn't have to be all bad," Jase said, drawing my eyes to him. His tone had softened.

"Shit," I muttered under my breath. "Can't you take me back with you at the next solstice?" I could agree to six months. That was reasonable. But forever? Uh. No.

"If only it was that easy. Our time is running out," Jase explained.

"What do you mean?" I asked.

Zade shifted forward, the leather groaning under his weight as he leaned his elbows on his knees. "We were only given a hundred years to break the curse—twenty years for each of us, including Tobias. Once the years run out, we are out of time."

A hundred years seemed like a long time. "How many years has it been?"

"Ninety-nine," Issik confessed.

I felt my blood go cold. What they were basically telling me was I was their last hope.

Damn.

They were screwed.

"B-but—" I stammered.

"Once the summer solstice arrives, the portal will never open for us again, and we will start to age."

Geez. No freaking pressure. My body was tense.

I thought living on the streets was tough, but this burden was possibly more than I could handle. "Why me? What made you think it could possibly be me? Other than I have blonde hair. Because if that is what you guys are basing your selections on, then no wonder you haven't broken the curse."

Kieran's lips twitched, but only his. Everyone else looked as if they wanted to wring my neck. "Jase has been our scout due to his ability. It's the easiest way to persuade possible candidates to the Veil."

Persuade my ass. "You mean by drugging them," I said straightforwardly. Harlow had implied the other girls had been brought here for the same reason and failed.

Jase cleared his throat, and I swung my gaze from Kieran to the purple-eyed shifter. "Something about you pulled me in. If you hadn't run into me, I wouldn't have given you a second glance..."

I scoffed. *Thanks for the backward compliment, asshole.*

"...but the moment I looked into your eyes, I felt it." His stormy gaze captured mine, and for a moment, a zing passed between us, and I knew what he was talking about. "You feel it too?" he asked, seeing the flicker in my expression.

"I don't know what I feel other than confused." I answered instead, shifting in my seat. "Everything that has happened in the last twenty-four hours seems more like a movie than reality." A really messed up movie.

Jase blew out an aggravated breath as if tired of rehearsing the same speech in this same room countless times. He probably had I realized. "I can assure you, we're very real. This place is very real. And the spell binding us is *very* real."

Tilting my head to the side, I was suddenly aware that these four gorgeous dragons had lived over a hundred years. "Just how old are you guys?"

Kieran cocked a crooked brow. "Before the curse? Nineteen."

My gaze appraised each one in turn, and I could see hope shimmering in their eyes, even Issik's. How could I let them down?

I was their last chance.

This was insane. It would crush them when they found out I was nothing more than a homeless girl.

But what else could I do except agree to help them as long as it didn't involve offering myself up as a sacrifice to the dragon gods? I had no idea where the Veil Isles were. No idea how to get home.

"What do I do?" I found myself asking.

The tense anticipation I didn't know existed in the room until now dissipated, the four guys visibly unwinding. "For now, just rest, relax, allow yourself to enjoy being somewhere safe," Jase said, leaning back in his chair.

If it were only that easy... Did Jase think he could just snap his royal dragon fingers and, like that, all my worries and fears would disappear? I could pretend to be on vacation? Have a little spa day? Read a book and swing in a hammock by the water? I must have snorted out loud, instead of in my head, because I drew curious glances from all four corners of the room.

"Sure. Whatever you say," I replied with a bite I couldn't mask, nor did I even really try to. "But after I'm done doing nothing but basking in the glory of being under the protection of dragons, then what?"

"You don't give up, do you?" Issik remarked, his tone like ice snapping.

"I like to know what crazy shit I'm getting myself into, especially if it involves my blood."

Jase blew out a breath. "Fine. Have it your way. On the next full moon, we'll take you to the place on the island that has traces of magic—the temple of our fathers. There we will perform the blood ceremony in hopes that it will remove the shackles that bind us."

Next full moon, huh? "How many days is that exactly?"

"Ten," Zade informed me.

Right. That made sense. The winter solstice had been last night, December twenty-first. It looked like I would be spending Christmas with a pack of dragons. I wondered if they celebrated holidays. I'd seen no evidence of decorations or anything festive in the keep, suggesting they didn't. Fine by me. I wasn't feeling much in the giving spirit. "What am I supposed to do until then? Twiddle my thumbs?"

"The castle is yours to roam as you wish, but only the castle. You won't step outside these walls." Jase's voice ended on a dark note of warning that I didn't understand.

"What is outside these walls?" I couldn't stop myself from asking. Anything forbidden immediately piqued my interest. I was the kind of girl who went looking for trouble unintentionally because I didn't like secrets.

Issik tipped his chin up, and the firelight sliced across his cheekbones. "That wraith last night was only a taste of the dangers you will find in the Veil." Caution punctuated his words.

But I was like a relentless child, always wanting to learn more. "How do I know you didn't say that to scare me into not running away?"

Issik's brow rose. "The wraith wasn't proof enough?"

Jase narrowed his eyes and folded his arms over his muscular chest. "Just stay put for ten days. None of us want to go chasing after you. We have enough to worry about."

It wasn't like they gave me much choice in the matter. I sunk into the fine leather couch, accepting that I wouldn't be leaving this place anytime soon. But after ten days, after they figured out I was not the one they sought, I *would* find my way home.

~

Jase escorted me back upstairs to my chambers, and this time, as we walked, I made a mental map so I could find my way back to the first floor. It would be wise for me to learn the layout of the castle and would undoubtedly come in handy one day.

We stopped just outside the doorway, and Jase's massive body seemed to relax. My skin tingled at his touch, when he invaded my personal bubble, brushing a stray strand of hair behind my ear. I tilted my neck to look him in the eyes, but the second ours connected, I realized my mistake.

"What is it about you that I'm drawn to? I can't figure it out." That made two of us. Something churned behind those stormy eyes, something that reached into my soul and wrapped around my heart, tugging me closer.

I didn't want to feel anything for my captors, and yet, my body didn't seem to share the same opinion. "It's probably the shampoo."

His chest rumbled against mine, reminding me how close he stood; my breasts tingled. His hand traced down my arm, making me tremble on contact.

Dear God. He is going to kiss me.

We stood with our eyes locked, and my breath stalled in my lungs. I didn't dare move for fear he would actually kiss me... or that he wouldn't.

"Go, before I do something neither of us would forget."

I blinked, dropping my eyes to the rich wood covering the hallway as the air whooshed out of my chest. *Did I want him to kiss me?*

I was afraid of the answer.

Before either of us did something stupid, I turned and slipped inside, shutting the door quickly behind me, just in case he decided to follow. Alone, I dropped against the wall, giving myself a few moments to collect my composure, and when I could properly think again, without a dragon shifter messing with my head, I contemplated what I should do: to run or not to run.

Sounded like Shakespeare.

My life did feel like a screenplay, tragic and dramatic, I had nowhere to go. And the unknown of what I would face outside the walls of the castle was enough to keep me in the confines of the four shifters... for the moment. I needed to get my bearings.

I nibbled on my lip, running the conversation through my head again. I had asked for the truth. Hadn't I? Staying was a risk, just as taking my chances out in the Veil were. Here, they could kill me. Serve me up on a silver platter as a sacrifice to the gods or Tianna herself—unlikely scenario, but then again, so were dragons. Or maybe it was all a ruse, and I was being punked. Or maybe I was reading the situation wrong. Or maybe this was the beginning of something monumental.

It didn't take long for a headache to form, my brain whirling. My mind churned over what would happen after the ten days were up. I told myself not to think about how they would react once they figured out I was no one special. For the time being, I was going to appreciate having a roof over my head, and food to eat.

Just think of it as a vacation, Olivia. One hell of a vacation.

Lying down, I closed my eyes only intending to rest for a few minutes, but I awoke hours later with the sun sinking over the western sky. I turned my head to the side, gazing out the glass doors. Orange rays brightened the heavens, casting the clouds in deep cobalt and bright turquoise.

A brief moment passed before the clarity of my situation seeped in. It didn't last but a few seconds, yet that was all it took for the pain of my life to come crashing down on me, which was then followed by everything else that had happened. I would never be back in my own room with Mom still alive.

Inhaling a deep breath, I rubbed at my eyes and sat up, swinging my feet over the bed. A tray of food sat on the little table beside me, letting me know I'd missed lunch. My stomach was used to skipping meals, but with the smell of something savory in the air, it rumbled. I lifted off the silver dome on the platter. A plate of bread and thin slices of meat laid waiting for me to enjoy. I tore off a hunk from the loaf and popped it into my mouth.

My gaze traveled around the room, really checking it out for the first time without fear or confusion distracting me. It was pretty, I guess—nothing grossly girly, but it had traces of a feminine touch. A fresh vase of flowers sat on the little wooden table beside the bed. Everything in the room looked handmade, from the sturdy oak bedframe, to the quilted white blankets wrinkled from my sleep.

I highly doubted Jase was responsible for the state of the room, which made me think the other girls here also helped keep up the castle. *Slaves. Maids. Victims.* The words rang in my head, and a surge of anger rose up inside me. I would be no one's bitch, certainly not to a pack of egotistical, unnerving, drool-worthy dragon shifters.

Why did my brain have to add 'drool-worthy'? Couldn't it have just stuck to their less than redeeming qualities?

Taking another piece of bread and a bit of salted meat, I stood up, needing to stretch my legs. Outside my door, a group of female giggles and whispers floated by. They passed on, and I was curious who they were. It might be a good idea to talk with some of the other girls… besides Harlow.

Testing the door, I was surprised to find it unlocked. Maybe they had been serious about me not being a prisoner, or they were the worst kidnappers in the universe. I stuck my head out, looking left and then right, sighing in relief when I didn't spot a mind-muddling dragon shifter keeping guard. Feeling pretty smug about sneaking out, I tiptoed into the hall, remembering the staircase was to the right. I edged around the corner, trailing my fingers along the cool, textured stones.

The voices carried down the stairwell, and I made sure to keep a safe distance. They were definitely female, but didn't sound the least bit distressed. How had they adapted so well to their situation? Being abducted and tossed aside when they were no longer needed wasn't something I could easily forget or forgive.

As I gnawed on my lip and had an internal conversation with myself about the stupidity of girls in general, I tripped over something that had no business being left on a staircase. I saw my life flash before my eyes. Who the hell left a shoe on the steps?

Holy shit. Oh shit. I'm going to break my neck.

Those were the thoughts repeating through my head as I started to fall forward.

A pair of arms swept around my waist, catching me before my nose hit the ground in a plummet that would have certainly shattered it. "And where do you think you're going?" asked a smooth voice that wrapped around me like a cloak of silk as he lifted me off my feet.

I didn't even bother to struggle. What was the point? The fire dragon, Zade, was superior in pretty much everything. "Nowhere. I was just doing some exploring."

Zade pressed his lips together, holding back a smirk that teased the side of my ear.

Asshole.

"It's probably not a good idea for you to go wandering off on your own." His breath was soft and warm on my neck.

My teeth ground together. "You mean you've been assigned to babysit me."

"Until the full moon, we agreed one of us should look out for you at all times."

"Wonderful," I mumbled under my breath, my feet still dangling as he carried me the rest of the way to the first floor. "So what? You just shadow me? Or do you also dictate where I go? And what happens when I have to pee?" I already knew what happened when I needed to bathe. They had no qualms about seeing me naked, and no respect for my privacy. Why should I have any for theirs? "Should I just follow you around like a puppy dog?"

His dark brows furrowed together. "You've made your point."

Then why didn't I feel victorious? I opened my mouth to say something smart that would have probably irritated Golden God, but my eyes shifted over his shoulder and I forgot what I'd been about to say.

I'd never seen anything so beautiful yet also wild and primitive. Through a pair of decorative doors was a circular courtyard showered with plants of vibrant colors and flowers as tall as me. Beyond the garden were the murky waters that seemed to surround the entire castle.

My feet were returned to the ground as I gawked, and I wandered outside, wanting to smell the exotic vegetation. "I've never seen flowers like this." The plants seemed to sing a gentle song that was ancient and hypnotic. It hummed around me, engulfing me in their fruity fragrance.

"Each region of the Veil has plants and trees that are unique to the land. The same goes for the wildlife."

I turned to see Zade watching me with a fascinated

expression. What did he see when he looked at me? "Including the dragons," I said with a smile.

His lips curved at the corners. "You're not like the others."

"You mean out of the gazillion girls you've stolen over the years, not one had a snarky personality?"

"Is that what you call it?"

Was this dragon shifter teasing me? I walked to the edge of the water and sat down on a dock, letting my feet hang over.

"I would think twice about sticking a toe in that water," he warned me, looming over my shoulder.

"And why is that?" I asked, swinging my legs in the air—the tips of my toes so close to the surface because I enjoyed doing the exact opposite of what he said.

Zade watched me intently, almost as if he was afraid I would accidentally fall in. He had valid reasons to be concerned. "We're not the only mythical creatures in the Veil Isles. Others are able to travel between realms, even in water."

He suddenly had my interest. My mind immediately went to my favorite Disney movie as a kid. "Like mermaids?"

His lips quirked as if he'd read my mind. "Not the kind you think, but in essence, yes."

I stared at the water with more intensity, pulling my legs up to my chest, no longer feeling safe. "Am I in danger here?"

"Always," he said, sitting beside me on the wooden platform, and our shoulders brushed. Heat seeped inside my body like a roaring fire during winter, and the bits of anxiety I had felt slowly faded. He had done that. There was something about these dragons that made me feel safe regardless of how I came to be here.

Why?

"Jase said you would protect me," I told him, needing reassurance.

"We will," he answered with a fervor I found comforting.

"How many other portals are there?" I asked, satisfied with his response.

"Many."

Not the straight answer I'd hoped for. "And mythical creatures?"

"Griffons. Sirens. Gargoyles," he rattled off.

"Gargoyles?" I interrupted, my voice squeaking in disbelief.

A frown marred his face. "Nasty little buggers. They can be quite violent when not in their stone form, and stealthy as fuck."

My eyes settled on the bright orange ball setting over the dark waters, and wondered what I would do if I came face to face with a gargoyle. I bet Harlow would squeal like the little girl she was. "What about all the other women you've brought here? What happens to them?"

Zade shrugged, his gaze following mine to the horizon where the sun was about to touch the gloomy waters. "They are given a choice to stay and live in any of our kingdoms, or the few who wish to return can do so during the solstices. Issik, Kieran, and I take them back."

He made it sound as if most remained, and I couldn't help but be inquisitive. If the Veil was so dangerous, why not return home? "Where are your lands?" I asked.

His hand lifted, pointing to the west where the shape of a volcano could just be seen through the misty fog. "The Crimson Keep sits just at the base of the Titan Mountain— the only volcano in the Veil."

A puff of smoke drifted up into the sky in the distance. "Just a guess, but is it hot most of the time in your domain? Not just the volcano," I added.

His eyes lit up. "Very."

The sunlight hit something in the water, making it

sparkle like glass through the mire. I couldn't take my eyes off the object that lay just a few feet from me. Like the garden, a lulling melody seemed to emanate from the waters, luring me closer. I placed my hands on the ground and leaned forward to get a better look. What was it? I wanted to touch it.

"Olivia."

I swore it called my name, and my hand reached out, itching to hold it in my hand.

"Find me, Olivia."

I didn't understand what was happening, only that I had to help.

Something splashed in the water near me, breaking the trance, and I more or less jumped into the dragon's lap. His strong arms came around me automatically, keeping me from falling into the water. "Olivia." Zade exhaled. "What happened? You wouldn't answer me."

"I-I don't know," I stammered. "I thought I saw something."

Frowning, Zade situated me more comfortably in his embrace. "The waters of Wakeland are not to be disregarded. They are dangerous as is most of the Veil."

Warning heard, and yet, I couldn't help but be intrigued. After one more glance, I turned to face Zade, finding him closer than I expected. I had forgotten I sat in his lap, and suddenly I felt his presence everywhere. His fingers on my waist made lazy circles over the material of my dress, leaving behind a trail of fire.

His already warm eyes flamed, and I couldn't look away. What was wrong with me? Ever since I stepped foot inside the Veil, I didn't recognize myself. But one thing I knew for certain, he was going to kiss me.

The simple brush of his lips sent a stream of heat spiraling through me, like a firework. It was a quick kiss, but it caused my entire body to come alive. When he pulled back, I leaned in toward him.

A hint of a playful expression crawled onto his face before he lifted me off, and brought us both to our feet, leaving me breathless. "Are you okay?" he asked softly, his cinnamon eyes bright as they searched my face.

I had just kissed a dragon. No, I wasn't okay.

The disturbing part was I wanted to do it again.

I never got the chance to reply, and my tied up tongue had only a part to do with it.

"What the hell is going on?" boomed a voice.

8

I leaped out of Zade's arms like I'd been burned with a frying pan... and maybe I had. My skin still radiated sparks.

Zade moved so he stood just slightly in front of me as if protecting me. Odd. Did I need protection from Jase? "Just making sure our little gem doesn't get herself in trouble." Zade cocked his head to the side. "Isn't that what we agreed on?"

The tranquility-breathing dragon stood inside the arched doorway, glaring at Zade with a mean scowl—his eyes so dark they almost appeared black. "Yes, but that doesn't include you seducing her."

"Since when do you meddle in my extracurricular activities?" Zade challenged him, with an edge to his voice.

It was my turn to frown. I was no one's extracurricular activity.

A growl rose up in Jase's throat. He stormed to where Zade and I where awkwardly standing. "She's off limits."

Golden God's lips formed into a tight line. "You forget, Jase, you're not king. There is no single ruler of the Veil anymore."

Things had escalated quickly, and I didn't want these two

going into the dragon ring over me. "Hey!" I yelled, stepping between the two. Not the brightest of ideas, but at the moment, it was all I could think to do. I didn't want blood spilled over me.

A muscle began to thump in Jase's jaw. "Keep your lips off her."

Spreading my arms out wide between them, my hands flattened on their chests. "Okay. First off, I can kiss whomever I want."

Jase's glower deepened.

I rolled my eyes. This was ridiculous. Framing Jase's face with both of my hands, I rose up on my toes and planted one on him, just to prove a point. The joke was on me.

The moment our lips met, all annoyance vanished from within me. My eyes fluttered closed as I fell into the blissful storm that was all Jase. His lips were soft... and skilled, expertly moving over mine. His hands came up to cup either side of my cheeks, and he deepened what was supposed to be a peck. My mouth opened, letting him in, and a purr sounded at the back of my throat as his tongue swept inside.

I'd never been kissed like this before—so passionately and fervently. My fingers bunched his shirt, holding him in place just in case he got any ideas about pulling away. I wasn't done yet. Honestly, I never wanted to stop kissing Jase Dior.

Zade cleared his throat behind us. How had I forgotten about him? Jase pulled back, his breath as ragged as mine.

I glanced up into his eyes, seeing the violet in them glowing brightly. "There. Are you satisfied?" I rasped, swallowing a knot of yearning. *No more kissing dragons.*

"Not nearly." Jase's head dipped as if he was going to take possession of my lips again.

My hand pressed against his chest, keeping him just out of reach. "Oh, no. I think I've kissed enough dragons today." I could barely believe I had locked lips with two of them within minutes of each other.

What is wrong with me?

Even more surprising, my little stunt actually had defused the situation… sort of. Their eyes no longer glowed, they took a step back, and their puffed-out chests relaxed.

"What do you have to say about not kissing her now?" Zade shot at Jase, looking damned pleased with himself.

Jase's spine straightened, and I thought for sure shit was about to get tense again. "No one but me gets the pleasure of tasting her."

Sometimes it sucked to be right.

Anger quickly returned to Zade's eyes, specks of gold flashing within them. "Hell no. I kissed her first."

I closed my eyes for a second, swallowing a stream of curses. "No one is going to kiss me!" I shouted before taking a breath. "I think I've had enough excitement for the day, and since I'm stuck here, I'm going to my room."

On my way back to the conservatory, I found Kieran leaning against the outer wall of the castle, watching the show with sparkling eyes. Issik stood next to him, frowning, his eyes like winter's first frost. I brushed past them, not saying a word, not even when Kieran stepped in time beside me.

Argh. I'd had my fill of hot-tempered dragons.

Ten days seemed like a lifetime.

Flying out of the garden and toward the stairs in the main hall, I made it two whole minutes before I broke my vow of silence. I'd never been able to keep my mouth shut, and that usually got me in trouble. My annoyed gaze traveled to Kieran, who still trailed me. "Why are you smirking?"

He raised his brows as we ascended the winding stairs. "Zade and Jase never fight. That was the most entertainment we've had in… well, years."

I didn't know if I was headed in the right direction, and was sort of relying on Kieran to make sure I got to the right room. "Glad I could be of assistance," I grumbled.

Devilishness glittered in his gaze. "I'm looking forward to seeing what happens next."

I rolled my eyes. "Don't get your hopes up." And I meant that beyond just my entertainment value. There was going to be buckets of disappointment when they all realized I wasn't *the one*.

"You might surprise yourself."

"Oh, I've had plenty of WTF moments since I got here." I wrinkled my nose.

He chuckled, pausing at a door I assumed was mine. "It's true, you know—what Zade and Jase said; there is something unique about you. I can't figure it out, but we all feel it, and it is the first drop of hope we've had in a very long time."

My face fell, displaying all the dread that had suddenly dropped into my belly like a boulder. A spark in Kieran's emerald eyes cautioned me to be careful. "Good night," I said before another dragon tried to kiss me.

"Good night, Olivia," he replied, winking.

Holy crap. What kind of dragon drama had I gotten myself into?

Shutting the door in Kieran's face, I went to lie in bed, staring at the painting on the ceiling. The artwork centered on an angel with glittery wings of gold. The midnight sky behind her was dark blue with pops of maroon and a thousand sparkling stars.

One thought circled in my mind before I dozed off to sleep. After the ten days, I had to find a way back home. Staying here with the four of them wasn't an option.

They can't keep me here forever. Not like those other girls. I'm not one of those girls.

～

Nine days to go… and so the countdown began.

I pulled open the drawers in my room, rummaging around for something useful. I wasn't sure what I needed, except for anything that might help me get out of here when the time was right. I hadn't given up on the notion of returning home. Not yet.

Nothing but clothes, extra blankets, and female essentials —including lotions, lip balm, makeup, and a toothbrush— were to be found. It alarmed me how the entire room had been set up for a woman. How many other rooms were there like this? How many other girls had stayed in this room?

To be frank, I wasn't sure I wanted to know. Sometimes ignorance was bliss. This might have been one of those times.

Sighing, I padded across the room and pushed open the double doors, letting in the morning sun and the gentle breeze, as it carried in the scents of honeysuckle and sea salt. There was no denying that the Veil Isles was a mesmerizing place. Water lapped against the keep's walls below, and in the sky, a flock of birds cawed.

Securing my hair in a messy bun with a black hair tie that I kept around my wrist like a bracelet—for emergencies—my attention was pulled to the gloomy waters, and like yesterday, I couldn't shake the feeling that there was something down there, something watching me.

I would have expected myself to be creeped out, but I wasn't. I was fascinated.

Walking back into the room, I stuck my feet into a pair of slippers, and reached for the doorknob to the interior of the castle. I twisted, once again relieved to find it unlocked. Stepping out into the hallway, I examined my door, trying to pick out something unique to help me find it again. Two sconces on the wall across from my room highlighted a couple of paintings portraying fierce, proud dragons. I made a mental note and crept forward down the corridor.

"A map would be damn helpful," I muttered, and cursed under my breath as I turned down another corridor before finding the stairs. But that wasn't all I found.

A pair of girls turned the corner just as I reached the staircase. They both appeared to be a few years older than me—early twenties if I had to guess. One had the most gorgeous olive skin color with warm honey eyes. The other was fair skinned, curvy, and had legs that went on for days. Their gazes fell upon me.

"You must be Olivia," the one with dark hair said.

"The keep has been buzzing about you," Legs added, a gentle smile tugging at her lips.

"Wonderful," I replied dryly.

"I'm Kaytlyn," the one with the envy-inducing olive skin introduced herself. "And this is Davina," she added, gesturing to the blonde.

Standing awkwardly in the hall, I wondered what I should say to them. I came up blank. "Where's the kitchen?"

They both blinked at me before Kaytlyn widened her smile. "We're on our way there now. We'll show you."

I almost didn't trust them being so nice.

Kaytlyn and Davina started the decline to the main floor with me behind them. "I remember my first days at Wakeland Keep. It was so intimidating, and I could never find my room," Davina admitted.

"This place is a maze," I agreed. "How long have you been here?" I asked, the question popping out of my mouth. I was curious about everything, but I probably shouldn't have assumed everyone was okay with divulging personal information.

"Four years," Davina answered.

"This will be my sixth," Kaytlyn replied.

Luckily for me, Kaytlyn and Davina seemed to be chatterboxes.

"And you've never wanted to go home?" This was the question I'd been yearning to know the answer to. Why did these women all stay?

Kaytlyn shrugged, her hand running along the mahogany banister. "At first it was a lot to take in, but you'll find living in the Veil is not so bad. I had nothing at home. Why not start over someplace new?"

And dangerous, I mentally added.

"They let you pick where you want to live afterwards," Davina divulged. Right. After they brought me to the temple of their fathers.

Our thin shoes clattered on the stone steps as we continued to descend the never-ending staircase. "You mean with one of the dragons." I was testing their reaction to the still foreign word. They didn't so much as flinch.

Davina nodded, her blonde curls bouncing. "Most of the girls choose Jase's or Zade's kingdom."

"And why is that?"

They both giggled. "Have you seen them?"

Oh, yes, I have. Was that all these girls cared about? That they were extremely attractive? "So, they're smoking hot," I agreed. "But what makes Jase and Zade different?" I didn't see how they could choose. Presented with the option to pick one of the four, I didn't know which one I would rate higher than the others. Except for Issik. He had a tough exterior, but maybe under all that ice there was a heart.

"I don't know where you lived before, but we didn't have guys like the descendants in Wyoming," Davina explained. "Besides, it's not just the guys, but also where they live. You just got here, but you'll see for yourself. The other kingdoms tend to be harsher climates and landscapes."

"You have nine days until the full moon?" Kaytlyn prompted me. I nodded. "Soon you'll be in the cave." Her voice carried in an eerie tone.

"What cave?" I automatically asked.

Kaytlyn batted ridiculously long lashes, watching me with an expression that said she didn't want to be in my shoes. "It's deep in the Viperus Woods of Kieran's kingdom."

She made the trip to the cave sound ominous, and I had to wonder if it was. "This is insane," I muttered. Curses. Dragons. Wraiths. What else could I expect?

Davina and Kaytlyn both nodded in agreement. "Yeah, it takes a while for that feeling to wear off," Davina confessed.

I wasn't positive it ever would, and I didn't plan to stick around to find out.

The kitchen was bustling with people—mostly females. Different types of stones lined the walls and floors of the industrial-sized space, and the ceiling vaulted into a dome, giving the room a circular appearance. In the center was a long rectangular wooden island with storage underneath. Food was spread out on the countertop, filling the air with both sweet and savory scents, waiting to be delivered to the tables beyond in the great hall. My stomach growled as I glanced over the fare, fighting the urge to pluck something off the buffet. The variety of brunch foods was different, yet familiar—a combination of fruits, eggs, and sweet rolls.

The lively chatter and shuffling died when I stepped into the kitchen, and all eyes swung towards me. I didn't like the attention or the silence. Then the whispering started, and I hated that even more, knowing everyone in the room was talking about me.

My back straightened, and I stiffened my chin.

"They're all wondering if you're the one," a cold voice whispered in my ear, sending a chill down my spine.

Issik.

My head turned a tad, finding him close. Too close. "What happens if I'm not?"

I swore I saw the corner of his lips twitch, but it could have been a trick of the light. "We won't let anything happen to you."

"Even after?" I pressed him.

He turned me around, so I looked directly into his icy eyes. "Yes."

I didn't know if I believed him, but what choice did I have in the matter? If this went badly in nine days, I would figure something out, because the only person who was going to truly look after me, was me.

"Olivia, you'll be eating with me and my brothers," Issik announced to everyone.

Thanks for singling me out, asshole. The last thing I wanted was to be treated differently or special. "Like I have a choice," I mumbled, my tone flat. I really just wanted to eat in my room, away from the prying eyes and the glances of pity.

His sharp, blond brow lifted. "You'll thank me later." He bent down, his breath cool on my cheek. Cold fingers wrapped around my elbow, causing a chill to climb over my arm, and spread through my body. I wanted to shiver, but I forced myself to stay still. Besides the coldness, I found it strangely comforting.

The soft material of the pink dress I had worn today, swished over my bare legs as Issik and I walked into the great hall from the kitchen together. Staci would have gone gaga over the color. Would I ever get the chance to see my best friend again?

Jase shot me a disarming smile, complete with dimples, as we joined his table, and my breath caught, wiping away every single coherent thought from my brain. "Good morning. Did you sleep okay?"

Ugh. How did he do that? And with just a smile? *A very sexy smile*, my sort of functioning brain reminded me.

It was too early to deal with all four of them, and I was beginning to regret leaving my room. I took an empty seat across from Zade and Kieran. Catching the scent of freshly brewed grounds, my eyes grew big. "Is that coffee?"

Zade nodded and began pouring me a mug. "How do you like it?"

"The stronger, the better."

Kieran wrinkled his nose. "Can't stand the stuff myself."

I took the warm mug with both hands and brought it to my face, inhaling. "I can't function without it. It smells amazing. God, I miss that."

"I'll make sure the kitchen has plenty on hand for you," Jase said, passing me a platter of what looked like diced potatoes with sautéed veggies.

Setting the mug down, I kept my hands wrapped around it for the heat to counteract the cold remnants of Issik's touch. "That's not necessary. I don't want to be any trouble. I'm sure I can manage brewing a pot when the mood strikes."

"If you change your mind, you only have to ask."

This feeling of being waited on was unsettling. I'd always envisioned having a massive house with cooks and maids to tend to my every desire would be glorious, but that wasn't how I felt at all. I didn't feel like a princess, regardless of my royal treatment.

"I won't," I assured him.

Forks clattered as breakfast resumed, and after piling a plate full, I took my first bite. The food tasted as exotic as the Veil, and I found it to be better, fresher, and more flavorful than earthly equivalents, including the coffee.

"Can I ask you a question?" Kieran said, eyeing me from

across the table. There was a glimmer of seriousness in his eyes.

"Sure, fire away." What did I have to hide?

"Why were you living on the streets? Do you have no family who cares for you?" He hadn't meant to drag up painful memories or judge me. I could see it in the softening of his eyes, but he was merely as curious about me as I was about them. And why shouldn't he be?

I swallowed. "I did have a family once. My mom... she was wonderful. She—" My voice hitched, getting stuck in my throat with the tears not far behind. "She got sick and passed away. I've been on my own since," I rushed out before I lost it.

"There's a reason you were brought here. You won't be alone ever again," Jase offered matter-of-factly.

Shit. They were going to make me embarrass myself. I wiped at my eyes, staring at my plate as I took a few minutes to gather my emotions.

Kieran captured my stinging eyes. "We've all lost those we care about."

It was true. The five of us all had parents pass away. We knew the pain of missing those close to us. Was that a coincidence?

A stirring wind came into the room, rustling the plants out in the courtyard and blowing the curtains covering the open doors.

"Tianna," Issik announced.

"It looks like we might be in for a storm," Zade added seconds before the screams began, and a flood of darkness took over. It descended upon the sky, wiping out any light. Instinctively, my body tensed as worry and unease set in. Something was very wrong.

"Blood bats," hissed Issik.

Uh. What?

Before I got the chance to ask what blood bats were, in swooped a swarm of flying creatures as black as midnight, with eyes that glowed like the fires of hell itself. My hands mechanically covered my head as I curled down to hide under the table. I felt fleshy wings brush my hair and squealed.

Nope.

I don't do bats, not of any variety.

My head hit the edge of the table in my scramble to get to safety. I was a disaster magnet. A hand flew to my head, to rub the now tender spot on my forehead, and I gasped at a quick pain that sliced over my arm. *Something bit me.* Forgetting about my head, I cradled my arm, feeling the warm, wet flow of blood.

The ground shook.

My gaze shifted outwards to find that one of the descendants had transformed. Zade. His dragon form was tall and fierce. His neck lengthened as he straightened to his full, glorious height. The scales covering his body were a deep red, almost brown.

Issik plucked me from my awkward spot, half under the table, and into his arms. "Hang on. Things are about to get toasty in here."

Bats circled the great hall with hunger in their beady red eyes. It was a damn good thing this room had vaulted ceilings. Actually, now that I thought about it, all the rooms in the castle had dragon-approved heights.

Zade crouched in the doorway to the courtyard—his tail inside and his long neck stretching outside. Opening his mouth, he expelled fire, lighting up the bloodthirsty bats trying to get in. Their shrieks echoed throughout the Veil, and I huddled deeper into Issik's chest.

The creatures fluttering inside the hall were rounded up

by Kieran and Jase. They herded them outside where Zade could finish them off.

"Are you okay?" Issik finally asked after what felt like hours, his cool breath blowing over my hair.

"What was that?" I breathed in choppy pants.

Issik unfolded his arms from around me, a troubling expression in his eyes. "A warning from Tianna."

Fear trembled on my lips. "Well, that wasn't very welcoming."

The ten days were up.

I woke knowing today was going to be a pivotal moment in my life. It would determine what happened next. If by some ridiculous odds, like winning the lottery, I was the one to break the curse, would they let me go home? And if I didn't release them from the spell binding them to the island, the same questioned remained. I knew I'd probably never get off this island, and as if the land had sensed my somber mood, the sky was blanketed in dark clouds, hiding any sunshine.

Doomsday.

That was what today felt like.

The four dragon descendants waited for me in the hall, pacing back and forth outside my door. I was surprised they hadn't just busted in, demanding for me to be ready. I understood their eagerness, but I was nervous as hell.

Soaking in a hot bath for thirty minutes had done nothing to soothe the tension in my muscles. What I needed was a Valium. Stalling wasn't helping my situation, so I gave up and headed to the door, taking one last look at the room that had become my sanctuary for the last ten days.

The descendants might have needed me, but I also had grown to need them… more than I'd anticipated. It made me realize how much I didn't want to go back to my old life. I wasn't positive that I belonged in the Veil, but I knew for a fact that the streets were no place for me either. After today, they were probably going to discard me like all the others. I wouldn't be special, and a part of me was more worried about being cast aside and alone, than not being able to break the curse.

With a sigh, I opened the door. The dragons' eyes swung toward me with a hopefulness that broke my heart.

Within minutes, I found myself outside the front gate of Jase's keep, boxed in on all sides by brooding dragon shifters. *Well, this is going to be a fun adventure.*

A gust of wind whipped across my face, and I gasped. Stretched out in front of us was an endless forest of towering pines, maples, and weeping willows that seemed to canopy the entire land.

Jase grabbed my hand and pulled me along while the others followed us down a dirt path that snaked into the woods. Pebbles scattered when our footsteps fell. We entered the vast woods, surrounded by tall trees and thorny thicket patches. Rocks lined the dirt pathway, which led us deeper and deeper into the forest, and I found myself drawing closer to Jase. I couldn't seem to help it. There was a malevolent ambiance among the trees that made me want to crawl under my bed. Jase's arms would have to do.

As if Jase sensed my uneasiness, he pulled me fully against him, twining his fingers around mine. All things considered, it really wasn't a bad place to be.

"Why do you get to hold her hand?" Kieran pouted.

"Seriously? Does it matter?" I argued. Each step farther in, felt like one step closer to my doom.

"Maybe," the green-eyed shifter replied.

Jase's smug smile grew, only irritating Kieran more. "I'm just ensuring she doesn't trip or fall. No blood spilled until we get to the cave."

How freaking considerate.

"We should take turns," Zade suggested.

Oh my god. Not him too. I rolled my eyes. "We're *so* not fighting about my hand right now." I snatched my fingers out from underneath Jase's, and a surge of anxiety rushed inside me. I stumbled. Holy crap. What was happening? My feet were suddenly paralyzed and refused to move.

"Olivia," Kieran called.

"She's scared," Issik groused. "Jase, take her hand again."

Once Jase's fingers touched mine, it was like a switch had been flipped inside me, taking away all my fear and reservations. I tilted my head up, glancing sideways at him. "You're using your ability on me, aren't you?"

His brows drew together. "Not intentionally." The others had stopped, and stared at us. "Let's go. We need to get there and back before nightfall," Jase grumbled.

I didn't bother to ask why the rush, because I knew I wouldn't like the answer. Nor did I ask why we weren't flying. The density of the woods would have made it difficult for a dragon, but the sky above seemed like a fast route.

"Here." I offered Kieran my other hand. "I've only got two."

Kieran happily took ahold of my fingers, interlacing ours together, and now I walked sandwiched between two dragon shifters. Joy. No escaping now—not that I actually thought I had a chance of doing so.

The five of us continued to hike through the jungle, and I couldn't help but notice how at ease Kieran seemed to be. I tried once to wiggle my fingers free from the two dragons, but neither of them budged, and I really didn't want them to start fighting again over who got to hold my hand. Things had finally settled down… for the moment.

After what felt like forever, I was about to demand one of them give me a piggyback ride when we came to a tree. Not just any tree. The biggest I'd ever seen in my life. I was talking Jack-and-the-Beanstalk huge.

My breath hitched as I paused to gawk.

"It's beautiful, isn't it?" Jase's voice was husky, sending a stream of comfort through me.

Damn tranquility dragon.

I just nodded, not bothering to scold him for screwing with my emotions, and leaned my weight against him, my legs weak from the trek. I'd never seen anything like the plant in front of me. The very old tree with a trunk the size of a house—probably bigger—had large exposed roots at its base that were interwoven with each other into a maze. They arched upward, forming an entrance over a round dark hole that dissolved into a musty cave.

"It's magnificent. Is it safe to go inside?" I asked. I wanted to explore, and it was too dark from outside to see the interior of the cave. Whereas the woods felt spooky and ominous, something about the cave called to me.

"Yes. It's safe. This cave has been here longer than the dragons," Zade explained in a voice like molten lava.

Peeling my eyes from the tree, I looked left and right to see that the descendants seemed as enchanted as I was. "What are we waiting for?" It wasn't that I was looking forward to what came next, but more so that I wanted to get it over with.

Kieran's lips twitched before he tightened his fingers, laced with mine, and drew me inside the cave, toward a pinprick of light flickering deep within.

The moment we stepped in its depths, I wanted back out, but I found myself rooted to the ground.

"What's wrong?" Kieran asked me, his green, luminous gaze falling on me when he felt my resistance.

Tugging my hands free, I wrapped them around myself. "Take your pick."

"There's nothing to be afraid of," Zade reassured beside me.

I snorted. Was he kidding? I could think of a dozen reasons off the top of my head, including the anger in their eyes when they figured out I wouldn't be able to release them from this curse. Taking a deep breath, I nodded.

We kept on a straight path, following the light, until it finally opened up to a clearing. I could see that the light was actually a torch embedded in a stone pillar—one of many that outlined the space. I stood on the outskirts, mouth hanging open. Five statues of men with beards, wrinkled faces, and hoods that draped to the floor were assembled near the center. Roots wove over our heads in an intricate network, and twinkling gold lights shimmered softly on the ceiling, like a million tiny stars. At the center was a rectangular altar with ancient marks carved into the stone, and on the ground surrounding it.

"What is this place?" My voice echoed through the open space, bouncing off the rock walls.

"It's the temple of our ancestors," Jase offered, his chest rising in pride, "and the one place on the island that generates mystic energy."

"Do you guys come here often?" I asked, curious who had lit the torches. My eyes were drawn to them.

Kieran stepped into the middle, the flickering lanterns illuminating only half his face. "No, only twice a year." He must have noticed my focus on the lights because he continued. "The flames are imbued with the curse. They will burn until it's broken."

85

"So, what now?" They'd gotten me here. That had to be the hardest part, or so I hoped.

Jase turned to face me. "We bite you."

I blinked. "I'm sorry, what?"

The four dragon descendants stood in a circle around me, and silence greeted my question.

Shaking my head, I backed up. "Uh. No. I didn't sign up for being bitten. Let alone multiple times."

Fingers lightly touched my waist. It was Zade. "Your blood is the key."

"Yeah, I got that part, but can't you just—I don't know— take a vile and drink it or some crap?"

Kieran's lips twitched. Issik folded his arms. Zade examined his nails. And Jase sighed. "We must be in our dragon form. It will only be a drop," Jase assured me.

"I must be freaking insane to even contemplate letting four grown-ass dragons bite me," I grumbled to myself, and then I looked each of them in the eye. "Where?"

Four sets of brows rose.

"Where are you going to bite me?"

The room filled with deep chuckles. "Anywhere you like," Kieran responded.

I blinked, ignoring the flush that stole over my body. "Fine. But make it quick." I held out my wrist. It seemed the safest part on me.

Their broad shoulders relaxed. "Up on the altar. Lie down," Jase instructed me.

All those visions I'd had ten days ago about being sacrificed to some dragon god came rushing back. I nibbled on my lower lip, uncertainty spiraling within me as I stood staring at the stone slab.

Jase cleared his throat behind me and touched the small of my back, immediately filling me with calmness. I spun, looking him directly in the eyes. "There's no need to fear us. We won't hurt you. I give you my word."

I nodded, keeping my gaze steadily on Jase as he helped me up onto the cold block. While he was coaxing me out of a mild anxiety attack, the other three had stripped, and suddenly the last thing on my mind was dying. There were four naked men surrounding me. My eyes didn't know where to look... or not look.

Each man was so different in his own way—from the tone of his skin to his unique personality. I didn't dare torture myself, so I closed my eyes and waited. The sounds were enough to keep my active imagination going. Bones, muscle, and skin stretched, grew, and adapted. The cavern was saturated with heavy breathing.

I felt the first sting of a bite on my arm as the first dragon sunk his incisors into my flesh, and with it a jolt of power surged in my body, causing me to suck in a sharp gulp of air. I tried to gather up every particle of bravery inside me. I had worked up about a tablespoon when all five of my senses were suddenly supercharged.

The musky air became more pungent, and I shivered as another pair of sharp fangs pierced my flesh lightly. Then another. And another. A groan escaped from my lips, and I bit down, tasting my own blood. It was then that my lashes fluttered open. Four dragons encompassed me, each of them with their radiant eyes locked on me.

A light flashed behind my eyes, momentarily blinding me, and my head fell back. This couldn't be normal.

What is happening?

Am I actually breaking the curse?

No fucking way.

When the light faded, I stared at a witch with flaming red hair and alabaster skin. She posed on the edge of a cliff—her hands raised to the sky, bolts of angry lightning crackling around her, five dragons circled above her head. I couldn't believe what I was seeing. Or how.

No one had to tell me that the figure I beheld was Tianna, the witch who had cursed the descendants. I was being given a glimpse of the past.

Her raven black dress unfurled behind her as the wind howled and raged. Even from a distance, I could see the pure, unadulterated hate in her eyes. She held a scepter in her outstretched arms, casting the curse and striking each of the dragons with magical light.

"No!" I screamed, but it was useless. The vision was of the past, and there was nothing I could do to change it.

Why I was being shown this moment? Did this mean I had something to do with breaking the curse? Or did all the girls before me see the same apparition?

As quickly as the vision had appeared, it faded, leaving me shaken while the effects wore off, and my vision cleared. I gritted my teeth. Jase, Kieran, Zade, and Issik were all huddled over me, no longer dragons. Worry creased their brows. "Was that it? Is the spell broken?" I croaked, my throat dry.

The four shared an equal look of dread and disappointment. "No," Jase finally spoke.

My stomach sank like the cave had collapsed. "Then what the hell was that? All the flashing lights and...stuff?"

"I don't know," Jase admitted, looking at the others for answers.

No one had any, but it was clear from their somber expressions, they had experienced the vision as I had.

Just freaking dandy.

"You mean to tell me that I'm not the one?" I said, sitting up.

"It doesn't appear so, blondie," Kieran said flatly.

If they hadn't looked like I just kicked their puppy, I

would have said, *"I told you so,"* but I wisely kept my mouth shut, remembering I had been their final chance at salvation. All of this was for nothing: my being kidnapped, trapped on a strange island, and doomed to spend my life as the girl who failed. I'd been their last hope; now they had none. They would die. And as I gazed into four pairs of very different eyes, a heaviness landed on my chest. I didn't want them to die. I'd only been with the descendants for a short time, but somehow they had weaseled their way into my life. I cared about them.

"I'm sorry. I-I don't know what to say," I mumbled, my emotions a tangled mess inside of me.

"It isn't your fault," Jase offered, trying to soothe my guilt, but it wasn't working, and when he reached for me, I pulled away because I didn't want him to take the dread I felt. If they were all suffering, why shouldn't I? He grunted, clearly displeased I wouldn't let him touch me.

"Dammit," Zade growled, and a moment later, his fist punched the side of the cave.

His display of self-pity—no matter how justified—only made me feel crappier. It also caused an avalanche within the cave. Pebbles and dirt rained down from the ceiling, flowing faster with each passing second. I lifted my hands over my head, but it offered little protection.

"We need to get out of here," Issik said, glowering at Zade.

Kieran slipped a hand around my waist, lifting me off the stone altar, and instead of setting me on my feet, he tucked me into his arms, shielding me from the destruction thundering down on us.

Even knowing I hadn't broken the curse, they still protected me. A lump of gratitude joined the fear inside me. Kieran hustled us into the dark corridor, and as we left the temple of dragons, I swore I heard a female voice laughing.

I twisted in Kieran's arms, glancing over his shoulders,

but there was no one there—no witch with devious eyes. *Great. Now I'm hearing shit.*

"What is it?" Kieran murmured in my ear as he picked up his pace.

Behind us a cloud of thick dust kicked up, and I hid my face in the space between his neck and shoulder. "I thought I heard someone," I admitted as the earth slowly settled as we moved closer to the exit.

"A female?" he asked.

I nodded, staring at his face. My eyes were drawn to his lips and the silver hoop. "How did you know?"

"Tianna taunts us often, but never the girls we've brought here."

I didn't want to think about the others who'd been here before me, not when he held me in his arms. He had a way of making me feel as if I was the only girl in the world. "She was laughing," I murmured.

His eyes slid to mine, and the usual mischievous gleam was missing from them. "I heard her too. We all did, but after a hundred years, you learn to ignore her. Reacting only gives Tianna what she wants, so we've learned."

We had reached the exit of the cave, but Kieran kept ahold of me, trailing just behind the other three guys. "You can put me down now," I urged, even as my fingers twirled the hair at the base of his neck. The truth was I was comfortable in his embrace.

His emerald eyes twinkled. "And if I'd rather not?"

"Kieran," Zade scolded him, spinning around and glaring at the other shifter with dark, narrowed eyes.

Kieran stopped and slowly dropped me to my feet, letting my body glide down his.

Damn.

The last thing I should be thinking about was his ripped stomach or how I missed the feel of him against me. As it turned out, I didn't get the chance to dwell for long on the way my body responded.

Zade flashed in front of Kieran's face, and I was shuffled to the side. "Will you stop pawing at her every chance you get?"

Kieran's answer was a cocky grin filled with trouble, just like him, which Zade retaliated by shoving Kieran in the shoulder. This was going to get ugly, fast, if someone didn't do something. My eyes sought out the other two dragons for help.

Jase and Issik had been walking shoulder to shoulder. They stopped to turn and see what the ruckus was now. Neither seemed surprised it involved me. "Should have known," Jase mumbled, crossing his arms, but did nothing to stop the hotheaded Zade or the troublemaker Kieran.

That left me. "Mother-freaking dragons," I muttered, stomping to put myself between them. Not exactly a safe place for a seventeen-year-old, who was only five feet five inches tall.

Kieran no longer grinned. The change in his eyes was like a viper, lethal and swift, as was his fist when it connected with Zade's face.

"Jesus," I breathed out for two reasons. One, if I had been any faster—thank God I wasn't—I might have been on the receiving end of that blow. And two, I couldn't believe punches were being thrown over me!

That had never happened before. Ever.

With my arms out in the warrior pose, I pressed my palms to their chests. This was becoming a much too familiar situation—me between two guys. I should be grateful it wasn't all four.

Fire leaped quickly into Zade's eyes. "Get out of the way, Olivia. I don't want you to get hurt."

"That wouldn't be a problem if the two of you stopped

acting like imbeciles," I argued, blowing a strand of hair out of my face.

Zade's response was to pick me up by my shoulders and move me off to the side, out of his way, but I wasn't having it and started squirming to break free. That was how I fell on my butt.

Fortunately, I landed on a patch of softly packed soil, instead of the twig beside me. I shuddered to think about… a stick up my ass. Wouldn't that have been my luck? Four concerned dragons hovered over me, all offering a hand. It was ridiculous—so much so that I started to laugh.

"Are you okay?" Jase asked, those violet eyes studying me with concern.

Breathless, I grabbed the side of my stomach and smiled.

The sky above us turned black, and I squinted, alarm suddenly chasing away the warmth in my cheeks. "Is that a—?"

"Wraith," Issik hissed, his cold eyes having followed the line of my gaze. He slipped his hand around my waist, pulling me to my feet. "We must get her to safety."

"Lead the way, Ice Prince." I winced. I hadn't meant to say that out loud.

He gave me a funny look, but my nickname for the shifter was the least of his concerns. The wraith screamed a sound that made my ears want to bleed, and its obsidian shadow fell over our heads, skirting the treetops. "Run!" Issik ordered me.

Shirts were flying off for the second time today as two of the guys immediately shifted and took to the sky. This was my chance to escape. I didn't know why the thought popped into my head at that moment, but once it was there, I couldn't get rid of the idea. I had made a promise to myself, if I didn't break the curse, I would find a way off this island. However, I hadn't factored in the feelings that had bloomed for the four descendants over the last few days. There might never come another opportunity like this when I was left alone, and if I had any real chance of going back to my world, I had to take it while I could.

But I'd underestimated the Veil and its penchant for danger. I had been warned, and I should have listened.

Running was something I could do. I might not be a track superstar, but these legs could sprint as long as there weren't fallen branches, tangled ivy, rocks, or basically anything I could trip on.

It just so happened that the woods were full of all the above.

Fricking awesome.

Did I mention it was also growing dark?

I was so screwed, but it didn't stop me from hauling ass. Sticking to the dirt path as much as possible, I headed deeper into the woods, uncertain where I was going. It wasn't long before my feet began to blister from rubbing against the slip-on. Branches and sharp leaves cut into my arms and legs, but I didn't stop, afraid of who would find me or who wouldn't.

Clenching my jaw, I bared the pain, and pushed forward. My heart beat rapidly from exhaustion and adrenaline, but through the treetops, I could hear the battle between the dragons and the wraith.

Out of nowhere, Kieran pinned me against a tree, shielding me with his body from the wraith that dove from the sky and through the treetops. Holy crap. Where had he come from? It was evident that Kieran didn't know his own strength. Pain seared through me, and I felt like a china doll that could shatter at any moment.

Everything about the dragon overwhelmed my senses, from the feeling of his muscular body pressed against mine, to the light scent of his woodsy aroma surrounding me. I could have easily forgotten the danger above.

His eyes swept over my face, and I stared back. "Are you okay?" he said.

I nodded, not trusting myself to speak.

"Stay here," he commanded me and then ripped his clothes off, shifting into a glorious dragon, taking off to help Jase and Zade in the sky.

Like hell I will.

My brain cells were just settling down after being shaken, when I pushed off the tree.

Finally, an opening came into view. Pale moonlight splashed onto the grass as I stumbled into the clearing, nearly falling and eating dirt. *That would have been a hell of a look, Olivia.*

I glanced around. Now what?

Did I keep running? Did I hide? And then what? I didn't know how to get off this island. I had been utterly foolish to think I could survive on my own. How long would I last out here? A few days? A week?

Five more minutes?

A twig snapped behind me, and I swung around, casting my eyes to the edge of the woods where I had come from. I found myself face to face with a wraith.

Holy shit! What's the plan now, smartass? Scream for help?

The shadowy creature shrieked, blowing my hair off my face. Its breath smelled of rotting flesh. *Someone needs a Tic Tac.*

Up close, the wraith was scarier than I'd imagined. Under

its hooded cloak of rags, the creature had no face. Where I expected to see his eyes was nothing but darkness. Completely freaked out, I sprang into action.

Turning, I ran, but I barely got a few yards before cold, bony hands latched onto me. Grabbing ahold of my wrist, the wraith wrestled me to the ground.

I hissed in pain as my head hit the ground. *Son of a bi—*

My breath evaporated as coldness stole into my lungs, snaking its way into my chest and throughout my body. I shivered. And I couldn't stop.

What was it doing to me? The world around me seemed to turn gray, losing all color, and my only thought was of death itself.

Paralyzed by fear or something else, I wasn't sure how long I lay there on the grass with the wraith on top of me. When all hope seemed lost and I could feel the life vacating my body, the wraith was suddenly ripped off me.

Still, I couldn't move.

I no longer felt connected to my body, unable to wiggle a toe or finger. Everything that made me human and alive was fading away, piece by piece. Growls and shrieks resonated in the clearing, and I knew my dragons were fighting the wraith. A white film had moved over my eyes, washing out the clarity of the world, just as someone sank to his knees beside me, and whispered my name. I thought I might have gasped, but I couldn't be positive it was me.

Sensing motion, I struggled to clear my vision and blinked rapidly. I was pulled into a man's arms—one of my dragons—but I didn't know which one, not until I felt the heat. He exuded heat like a bonfire. Zade. The fire dragon cradled me against his chest, and slowly the feeling came back into my fingers, my toes, and my lungs. My hands buried themselves into the hair at the nape of his neck, and I pressed my cheek against him, the coldness inside me melting into the warmth of him.

But it wasn't enough. I opened my mouth to tell him I needed more, but I didn't know what to ask for.

"Shh. Don't speak," he whispered in a terse baritone.

I could just barely make out the features of his face, but I took comfort in it, thinking I might not die after all.

Zade gently pressed his thumb to my chin, prying open my jaw and placing his lips to mine. This wasn't exactly the perfect time to make out, but once his soft mouth touched mine, it was all I wanted. Heat filled my body, and I finally understood what he was doing. His dragon's breath burned inside me, chasing away the lingering effects of the wraith.

His lips remained pressed against mine until they tingled. Everything tingled really. Zade pulled away. "Are you okay?" he asked.

"I-I think so, but don't let me go just yet." I still felt a little wobbly, but that could have been from his kisses.

"I wasn't planning on it." He brushed the hair off my face, keeping me tucked into his arms. "I'm used to girls freaking out, but you're not going to faint, are you?"

I wasn't planning on it either.

Much to Zade's disappointment, I didn't faint. Three naked dragon shifters stood around me. Thank God Zade had clothes on, because that would have been the height of my embarrassment. I didn't know what to say. "Are you guys always naked this much?" I mumbled, the words popping out of my mouth.

"Does it bother you?" Kieran countered as if the idea of spending more time in the nude with me appealed to him.

"How do you feel?" Jase asked, ignoring Kieran.

"She's… annoyed," Zade answered, while staring at me with a thoughtful expression.

How could he possibly know that? I wasn't miffed at them, but me. I had almost just died, and all I could think about was the four glorious shifters surrounding me—proof I needed my head checked. "And how would you know what I'm feeling?" I directed my question at Zade.

"I don't know. I sensed it." He rubbed at the center of his chest like what I was feeling was right there inside his heart.

"Is that something you guys do?" *And failed to tell me about*, I added silently.

"No," answered four unanimous, deep voices.

I was willing to brush it off. It didn't seem like that big of a deal since it was pretty common to read people's emotions. And then this happened.

"Okay, you've had her enough. Give her up." Kieran reached for me.

I still sat in Zade's lap, and although it had slipped my mind, it didn't get past Kieran's attention.

"Don't get possessive. She's ours to share," Jase answered, pulling on a pair of jeans but leaving the top button undone as he bent to pick up his shirt off the ground.

Since when did I become *theirs*? I wasn't having it. "You guys don't own me. I'm not anyone's. Especially not until you put some clothes on."

"The four of us are responsible for you now," Issik spoke up for the first time since the wraith attack. I was glad to see he had put on clothes... mostly. He was still shirtless.

I rolled my eyes. "And what does that mean? You're going to pass me around like a joint to share?"

"She's angry now," Zade said, studying me oddly.

Do I have something on my face? Why is he looking at me like that? "I have a right to be upset. I've traipsed through the woods, been pulled into a cave at the bottom of a tree trunk, been bitten four times by dragons, and attacked by a wraith. I'm waiting for my freaking badge of honor."

"Yep. She's pissed," Zade added. "I can feel her irritation rolling like waves. It's making the fire inside me roar."

The other three dragons all turned sharp eyes on Golden God. "What do you mean?" Jase demanded.

Zade forked a hand through his hair. "I don't know. It's like her anger is a part of me, simmering in my blood until it starts to build inside her."

"Here, let me try." Kieran pulled me to my feet and into his arms. Before I realized what he was doing, his lips were moving over mine. I touched his cheek and closed my eyes. I might be a virgin, but I'd fooled around before, and the venomous dragon knew how to work those hot lips. I sighed, leaning into him. My knees felt weak.

Kieran broke off the kiss, staring down at me with moonlight in his eyes. "I felt it too," he said, wide-eyed, rubbing the same spot on his chest that Zade had.

What is going on?

"Well, of course *you* felt something," Jase growled. "You just kissed her brainless."

Kieran sucked on his lower lip like he wanted to savor the taste of me. "It wasn't just chemistry, which there was plenty of. I could feel her passion inside me."

Zade had straightened to his full height and glared at the green-eyed dragon shifter. "What the hell. Why does he get desire?"

Seriously. Were they now arguing over my emotions? What next?

I stepped out of Kieran's arms before he decided to plant another one on me to test his theory some more.

"She might not have broken the curse, but something definitely happened in the cave." The silky smoothness of Kieran's voice had disappeared altogether, replaced by deep concern.

"I agree. When the wraith showed up, her fear was so

strong inside me, all I could think about was finding her," Jase admitted.

My hands dropped to my hips, and the bitch came out. "Wait. A. Freaking. Minute. Are you telling me the four of you can now feel my emotions?" Oh, hell no.

"It's possible something happened when we took a drop of your blood," Issik concluded.

Please tell me this is a joke. I shook my head. "This can't be real. So I didn't break the curse, but I managed to emotionally entangle myself with four dragons. Jesus. How does this crap happen to me?"

"She's sad," Ice Prince said, looking at me strangely.

"Okay. Enough! Stop." I backed away from the four of them, not wanting any of the dragons to touch me. "I don't want to think about this anymore. I'm exhausted. Can we just go home?"

Home.

The word echoed in my head. Home was Chicago, not Jase's castle, yet it was the room in Wakeland Keep I had been referring to. This wasn't my home, I reminded myself, I couldn't forget it. This was only supposed to be temporary, but from the sound of things, the descendants weren't going to let me leave.

"She's right," Issik said. "We need to get her to safety before anything else shows up."

I didn't like his intimation of other things. Hadn't the wraiths been enough? What creatures should I be worried about, besides the four dragon shifters eyeballing me? I was getting sick of them constantly sharing glances that had double meanings. What were they keeping from me?

"Can you guys put the rest of your clothes on? Button up the pants. Throw on a shirt. It's very distracting." My eyes couldn't stop straying to certain parts of their bodies. I hadn't seen enough naked men in my life to judge what qualified as va-va-voom, but the dragon descendants had all the working parts.

"We're making her uncomfortable," Jase said.

Argh. This emotion-sensing thing royally sucked ass. I'd never be able to hide anything from them again. *I don't think they're sexy. Not one single bit,* I told myself. "They're not sexy," I accidentally let slip out. My hands flew to my mouth, and I groaned. Tell me I had not just mumbled something about being sexy out loud. I glanced up at four very smug dragons and groaned again.

Damn them.

They were going to be the end of me.

Zade crossed his arms and gave me a look. "What are you muttering about?"

My hand pushed through my messy hair, but it was a failed attempt. The numerous knots made it impossible to manage. "Nothing. It's not important."

Issik strode back into sight, his jaw locked.

"Do the four of you ever get along?" I asked.

"Yes," four deep voices answered together.

"Well, at the moment, I'm finding that hard to believe."

"Come on, Cupcake," Jase said as he started to move, taking me along with him. I didn't even bother to fight him. Maybe I was becoming used to being manhandled by the four of them.

I waited until we left the clearing and ventured back into the woods before peppering them with more questions. "What did it want?" I inquired about the wraith.

"You," Jase said in a very low voice.

Kieran slipped in next to Jase. "The wraiths are the dead of the Veil—our kings, our queens, our mothers, brothers, sisters, and fathers. Tianna's spell prevents them from moving on. They are as tied to the island as we are."

What was her deal? Why had she gone to such great

lengths to curse the descendants and the island? There had to be more to the story. The dragons all walked with long, purposeful strides that I more or less had to run to keep up with. "What did it do to me?"

Jase's jaw grew tight, his cheek ticking. "Wraiths feed on humans, stealing their souls. They know why we brought you here and will do anything to stop the curse from being lifted at Tianna's command."

"But I didn't break the curse, so why would it try to kill me?" I asked, kicking a rock in my effort to stay with their pace.

Jase didn't answer at first, and I couldn't help but wonder if they were going to constantly keep me in the dark. How frustrating. I was here because of them and their stupid problems. The least they could do was tell me the truth.

"Because all hope isn't lost," Jase finally answered.

"I don't understand."

"The attack on your life, however distressing it may have been, means there is still a way to sever the tie that binds us to the island. You're the key; we just haven't figured out how you unlock the curse yet."

"So I gave you my blood for nothing?"

"Not nothing. You can't forget the link to your emotions," Kieran so kindly pointed out.

Again. That wasn't something I was happy about. "Is there anything else I should know about this spell?"

"There is one other thing," Jase confessed.

"Don't hold out on me now," I retorted.

Zade glanced down at me, a flash of anger in his eyes. "It also forbids us from siring children. If we don't find a way to break it, the dragons die with us."

So it wasn't just about their future, but also the fate of their race. "What do we do now?" I asked.

Jase shook his head. "There must be something we're missing, something we haven't thought of. And your blood..."

"What about my blood?" It drove me crazy when people didn't finish their thoughts. I didn't like suspense.

"None of us have ever tasted blood like yours. You are different, but it was more than the sweetness of it, it was as if you became a part of me," Zade finished. His body was still lined with anger, but the resentment wasn't directed at me.

"And the wraith's attack on you only proves it," Issik added.

So it wasn't just Jase who felt this way. None of them had given up.

"Tianna has the wraiths guarding the boundaries of the Veil. If they are hunting us, then we are doing something right." I could see flickers of fire and the promise of revenge in Zade's expression. He wanted Tianna to pay for what she had done to them.

My hand extended, and I found myself reaching out to touch the closest dragon. It was Issik. He stared down at my fingers. "Let me guess, this is going to be very dangerous, isn't it?"

The four of them shared one of their famous looks. "Yes."

"But we swear on our lives, we will protect you." Kieran rushed to jump in, and smooth over the mounting anxiety that had built in my chest.

I believed them. They had as much to lose as I did. Probably even more so. "Anyone have an idea of how to break this curse? This bitch is going down."

They rewarded me with four grins of pure sin. My dragons.

No. Not *my* dragons.

I was just helping them, and once we unwove the spell

Tianna put on the dragon descendants, I would get on with my life.

Whatever that meant.

And my delusions of the future ran amuck in my head.

The journey back to the keep wasn't as treacherous as the trek to the cave had been. We picked our way through the woods, winding down the same path we had traveled earlier in the day. I started to lose steam quickly, lagging behind and tripping over my achy and exhausted feet.

After the third time of stumbling over a branch, Jase slipped an arm around my waist. "Hold on to my neck," he murmured, waiting for me to lift my arms.

"I can walk," I insisted, concentrating on putting one foot in front of the other.

"Are you always this stubborn? And clumsy?" he added.

My head whipped to the side and I glared. "I am neither stubborn nor clumsy."

He smirked, and I knew I was in trouble, not the life-threatening kind, but the why-does-he-have-to-use-those-dimples-on-me kind. "Good. Then you better hang on." Jase didn't give me a chance to argue. Dipping his shoulder, he put an arm under my legs and lifted me up.

I crossed my arms at first, refusing to give in, but it was awkward, leaving me no choice. My hands slipped around his neck.

Minutes later, my head became too heavy and I could no longer resist the urge to rest it on the space between his shoulder and neck. I sighed softly, comforted by the calming scent of him. Like the sound of the sea, he lulled me to sleep. I was pretty sure he'd used his tranquility on me, but I was too tired to care, especially when he suddenly brushed his lips over the side of my cheek. My fingers tightened at the nape of his neck as a surge of tingles danced inside me.

It was nothing. Just a simple kiss, and yet it felt anything but simple. If I wasn't careful, these four dragons would find a way into my heart. I didn't know how I could feel so equally attached to them, but there was no denying something definitely was brewing between us. Just what was I going to do about it?

My eyelids fell closed, and they didn't open again until my arms were wrenched off Jase's neck. He laid me down in my bed as I glanced up at him from half-lidded eyes. I rested a hand on his arm, not wanting him to leave just yet. "Are we home?" I asked groggily.

He sat on the edge of the bed, the mattress shifting to one side under his weight. "Yes, and it would be in your best interest if you stayed inside. No more escape attempts."

My fatigue vanished. I opened my mouth to say something in my defense and then quickly snapped it closed. How had he known? For all intents and purposes, I could have been just running aimlessly in the woods.

"The wraith has your scent. He'll be back with others too, and you're going to need our protection, Cupcake."

Shit.

Well, that just sealed the deal, didn't it? Jase gave me no choice. If I tried to run again, the wraiths would probably find me first. "Fabulous," I muttered sarcastically.

His finger brushed along my jawline, lingering just over

my bottom lip. "Try and get some sleep. One of us will be near."

Was that supposed to provide me comfort? It didn't. Just the opposite. My entire body erupted in a heat similar to when Zade had blown his breath into my lungs. "How near are we talking? Like in my room?" The coloring of my cheeks morphed in the darkened room, and his eyes were drawn to them.

He grinned. "If you like."

Did I want him in my room?

I was afraid of the answer. "Is there a bed big enough for five?" I joked, but the gleam in his eyes made me sorry I had.

He raised a single brow. "Are you into that kind of thing?"

"No," I exhaled on a nervous laugh. "Definitely not."

"You sure?" he asked, trailing a hand lightly down my arm.

At the moment, I was only into him, but I shook my head, giving him the truth. "No. I can't explain it, but I'm all mixed up inside." And then there was the fact that the four of them could sense my emotions. I still hadn't digested that clusterfuck.

"Maybe I could help you clear things up."

The mischief in his eyes told me his idea of "clearing things up" would only complicate matters more and entangle my feelings deeper in the web woven by the descendants. *Don't look at him. Keep your eyes glued to the bed.*

"Look at me," Jase murmured.

His velvet voice pulled at me, and I lost the battle. Staring into his smoldering deep purple eyes, I held my breath and waited. He leaned down, a lock of dark hair cascading over the side of his temple.

My heart started pumping, and my fingers dug into the bed. He was going to kiss me. Dipping forward, my eyes drifted shut, and that was when I felt his mouth brush the tip of my nose. He sat back, a smile teasing his lips, and in the moonlight, I saw a flash of dimples.

Argh. He really knew how to torment a girl. My grip relaxed against the sheets as I exhaled and struggled with the desire to pull him to my lips. What did that say about me? I should be running far and fast from Jase Dior.

But I couldn't.

And from the smug grin on his face, he knew it. The jerk probably had kissed every girl here.

The thought was like being thrown in a bath of ice-cold water. My eyes hardened, and I pushed at his chest so he no longer leaned over me. "I'm not your current plaything, and that goes for all of you."

Irritation reflected clearly across his face. "Why would you think that?"

"You have a house full of girls just like me." They had been special at one time.

His expression turned to stone, masking any emotion. "The thing is, Olivia, none of them are like you."

"How do I know you're not just telling me what I want to hear?"

"For one, it's the truth. And two, we've never had a connection to anyone before." His hypnotic voice placated me.

How could I forget for even a second our emotional five-some? "I just don't want to be screwed with," I confessed.

What I really wanted to do was demand to know how many of the girls he had kissed, how many he had slept with. Jealousy was an ugly feeling, but the vision of my dragons with other girls sent me into a tizzy. Ten percent of my frustration could be attributed to exhaustion, but the other ninety percent was all possessiveness.

"I don't know what is going on in that pretty head of

yours, but I'm not just being a flirt. The way I feel about you is serious," he murmured.

How do you feel about me? I asked inside my head but couldn't bring myself to say the question out loud.

Jase tucked the corners of the blanket around me so I was cocooned in the bed. "Now, get some sleep." Standing up, he walked out the door, leaving me alone with my thoughts.

Which was a scary place to be. Almost as scary as the wraiths.

Feelings were weird.

Back in the real world, I'd never really had a boyfriend. I had dated a little, then Mom got sick and my love life no longer mattered. But when I looked at Jase, Zade, Issik, and Kieran, there was something unique about each of them that I found endearing. The four dragons struck different chords inside me.

What made me feel so possessive of them? Was it because they were dragon shifters and I'd never met anyone like them? Did they exude some kind of pheromone attracting me to them? That would make sense, but this need to be near them, to touch them, and do things to them that would have made my grandma blush, didn't make sense.

They had kidnapped me, and here I was thinking about their lips.

All four sets of them.

I had to think about this for a moment. What was I saying? Four?

That was quite a lot of dragons to handle, yet I couldn't choose one over the other. But I was totally getting ahead of myself. They might not even think of me as anything more than a means to an end—their freedom. So what if they had kissed me? Well, Issik technically hadn't—the only one of the four who had shown any restraint. Or maybe it was just lack of interest, but at times, he seemed to care about my well-being. That had to count for something, right?

My mind continued to make excuses on his behalf, until a new thought struck me.

What would happen if I somehow, by a million-to-one shot, managed to free them from the curse? Would they discard me like the other girls then? Would that be a bad thing?

Yes. The thought of living in the same house as one of them, and being cast aside as just another girl, filled me with dread. From the moment I'd arrived in the Veil, they had made me feel special, and I liked sitting on the pedestal they'd created. What did that say about me?

As I lay in the dark, my memory recalled each of their faces and how distinct they were.

Jase, with his dimples and calm disposition, was the level-headed one the others turned to, even if they didn't realize it. A natural leader.

Kieran, the fun-loving and light-spirited dragon, had a wicked side to him that I was dying to unleash. The lip piercing, the tattoos, and those luminous green eyes spelled danger.

Zade, everything about the golden gold was hot, from his body to his soul. But he had a quick temper to match the fire in his eyes.

Issik, my ice prince—guarded and quiet. But under that frozen exterior was a heart waiting to be thawed. I surprised myself by wanting it to be me who would get him to open up.

Dear God.

I was falling for them. For all of them. How did that even happen?

Four guys. One girl. They would never go for that, would they?

Shaking my head I rejected the idea. No. They were

proud and selfish—especially regarding me—but they were "sharing" me as they so eloquently had put it.

Just maybe...

I was insane. This wasn't happening. *Stop fantasizing about these dragons and start devising a plan to get the hell off this island. You still want to go home, don't you?*

That was the thing. Everyone had warned me I might like it here, but yet, I hadn't believed I would ever consider staying in the Veil Isles. The truth was, I didn't want to go back to the streets of Chicago. To the cold, harsh winters. To being alone. To fighting for my survival each day.

My life in Chicago hadn't been easy.

What did I have to lose here in the Veil?

The answer... nothing.

This could be my chance to start over, and do something meaningful with my life. It wasn't the life I'd imagined, but that didn't mean it had to be any less significant.

The image of four dragons, wrapped around me like a warm security blanket, engulfed me as I drifted off to sleep.

I'd been cooped up inside for two days, and I was seconds away from throwing myself off the balcony, just to see which dragon would save me. My boredom had reached that crazy level where I was dying for excitement of any kind.

There was no TV. My cell phone didn't work in the Veil. And the four dragons that were keeping me captive in this room hadn't bothered to show their faces.

I hated being ignored. They were up to something, but I didn't know what. Why else would they disappear?

Maybe they are bored with you.

Maybe they don't need you after all.

Maybe my insecure self should just shut the hell up!

I finally got fed up with the silence, and went looking for *them*. I found Davina, Harlow, and Kaytlyn instead.

The three girls cornered me outside of Jase's office, which I had been about to barge into unannounced, and demand to know that he tell me what was going on.

"Everyone is talking about you," Harlow said as my hand reached for the doorknob.

I spun and pasted the biggest fake smile on my lips. "That's nice," I replied snappily. "Have you seen them?"

"*Them?*" Harlow drew out the word with a smile that was anything but nice.

Gag me. Girls like her used to make me sick in high school. "Yeah, you know, the four assholes who kidnapped us."

Kaytlyn snickered. Davina's hand flew to her mouth, and Harlow sneered. At least I had gotten a reaction out of them. This was the most interaction I'd had with people in days. "Are they ignoring you already?" Harlow tsked her tongue. "I guess the rumors aren't true then." She looked loftier than a cat who had just eaten the mouse.

I crossed my arms and planted my feet firmly on the ground in case things turned south. The fire in her eyes told me she wanted to go a round or two with me in the ring. And based on how I currently felt, I would welcome the release of anger. I angled my head to the side. "The one about the descendants being linked to me? It's true. You never know what will happen when you give someone your blood." My bitchiness had reached new heights and it was all *their* fault. Damn dragons.

Harlow stuck up her nose. "That's not what I heard."

"Then I guess you don't have a reliable source."

"But the curse hasn't been lifted," Davina pointed out, but not in a cruel way like Harlow would have. She sounded genuinely curious.

I shook my head. "No, but something else happened."

"We wondered what all the secrecy and commotion was about," Kaytlyn added, and was rewarded with a jab in the gut by Harlow.

So I wasn't the only one who'd noticed things were weird. "What commotion? Where are they?"

Harlow shrugged. "Gone."

"What do you mean 'gone'?" That didn't make sense. Jase had said they would protect me, that one of them would always be near, and yet here I stood… alone. My face fell, and I regretted the moment of vulnerability I'd revealed to Harlow.

Her expression was filled with smugness. "They all left two days ago. The night you came back."

I wanted to call bullshit, but from the looks in the other girls' expressions, she wasn't lying. Why would they leave? Where did they go? How could they abandon me without even saying goodbye?

"It was bound to happen. They tend to lose interest pretty quickly once they get what they want," Harlow gladly gloated.

She was lucky there were witnesses; otherwise, I would have popped her in the face. I wondered how pretty she would look with a broken nose. "I wouldn't be so sure about that." I was being cocky. I only hoped it didn't come back to bite me in the ass.

Flipping her hair in a dramatic fashion, she appeared indifferent. "Suit yourself. I was just offering a bit of friendly advice."

Ha. She didn't know the meaning of friendly. We both knew she didn't give two shits about me. "Don't you have someone else to intimidate?"

The smile that crossed her lips was one of victory. She'd gotten what she wanted—to get under my skin.

Drawing in a breath, I turned around, twisted the knob on the door to Jase's office, and stepped inside. The room was so quiet; the only sound was the water lapping outside. I inhaled deeply, taking in the scent that was all Jase—wild summer nights and ocean spray.

Curling into the deep leather couch, the smooth fabric cooling my cheek as I lay down, and tucked my hand under a knitted pillow. I felt crushed, and I couldn't even rationalize why. From the moment they had flown into my life, my mind had been scrambled. It was all so much, and for the first time since I arrived in the Veil, I broke down. Tears I couldn't stop fell, streaking down my cheeks as I stared at the empty office. I lost track of time, but hours must have passed, and soon my eyelids grew heavy. It became a struggle to keep them open, and eventually, I closed my eyes.

For the first few seconds upon awakening, it felt like a fantasy—not sure of my surroundings—and then it all hit me. Dragons were real. I had some kind of emotional link to four of them, and for some reason beyond my comprehension they thought I could save them.

What a joke.

But it wasn't. This was my life.

I hadn't opened my eyes yet, still lingering in the dregs of sleep. Something tickled my nose, and I brushed it aside, not ready to face another empty room, but the feeling was persistent. I swatted the air near my face, and hit the tip of my nose. Snickers from around the room had me cracking one eye open and then the other.

I was no longer alone in the room, and the descendants were in deep shit.

"Where the hell were you?" I yelled at the four of them, bolting straight up on the couch as I shoved long strands of honey hair out of my face.

"She's mad," Zade said, smiling. He leaned against the wall, feet crossed at the ankle.

Four sets of eyes observed me, each sparkling different

colors in the dark room. The hearth had been lit, and the wood crackled, casting a warm glow. "Damn straight I'm mad. You guys just LEFT ME."

"We have kingdoms that needed our attention." Issik exhaled as if irritated, but his eyes seemed to soften when they looked me over. He was the closest, sitting on my couch, while Kieran stretched out on the other sofa.

Fine. I understood they had responsibilities, but Jase? This was his home. "Where were you?" I asked him directly.

He folded his hands together on top of his desk. "Searching for answers."

"And just where the hell does a dragon go looking for clues about breaking a curse?" I was being a smartass, but I couldn't seem to stop myself. I was so relieved to see them, to know they were safe, but that relief had quickly turned to anger.

Issik's stunning features pinched together. "She's still pissed. Jase, do something to calm her down."

My hands shot up in the air. "Oh no. Don't you dare think about using your tranquility mojo on me."

"What are you doing in here? Did something happen while we were gone?" Jase asked, but I could tell by the darkening of his eyes, he wanted to ease my aggravation.

Yes. You left me here. That's what happened. And I think I missed you. But that wasn't what I said. "You told me one of you would be near, and then you all just disappeared. How am I supposed to trust anything you say?"

"We didn't want to disturb you—not after the day you'd had at the temple, and the attack from the wraith. We thought it best that you stay here and rest. Jase was supposed to—" Kieran realized what he was about to admit and quickly stopped himself.

I swung my glare of outrage to Jase. He was supposed to have tranquilized me. "You didn't," I accused him.

His brows drew together. "Does it matter? It clearly didn't work."

That wasn't the point. I frowned and sunk back into the couch. I tried to calm myself down before I did something drastic, but I couldn't erase what Harlow had said to me. "Do you guys get off screwing with me?" I mumbled to myself—an increasingly annoying habit.

"You make it far too easy, Cupcake." Jase flashed his wicked dimples to defuse my anger. "There is no need to be upset."

Says the guy who has an innate calmness. "Am I supposed to just sit here and pretend you can't tell what I'm feeling?" I asked. "You guys can't mess with my emotions like that."

Zade grimaced. "It was only our intention to keep you safe."

No longer able to hold onto my anger, I fumbled with the yellow dress covering my legs. "Did you find anything out about the curse?"

"She's worried now," Issik announced. No one answered my question.

I rolled my eyes. "You guys don't need to announce my every emotion. I know how I'm feeling."

Kieran didn't miss a beat. "But *we* want to know."

It was bad enough one of them would always feel what I was feeling. Now they had to share that information as well. We were going to nip that in the bud right away. "Some things are personal—emotions being one of them."

"Have you not learned to trust us yet? Have we not kept you safe?" Kieran questioned me. I wasn't sure what that had to do with my feelings, but I assumed they thought I didn't believe in them enough to protect more than just my body.

Did I though?

Zade shifted his stance against the wall. "Besides, we like

knowing what you're feeling. It's the first real thing that has happened on this island in a hundred years."

"Glad I can be of service," I grumbled. So much for trying to get them to see my side of things. Ugh. Damn headstrong dragons.

Jase sat on the table in front of the couch and crossed his arms. "My staff told me that you barely left your room."

"You're spying on me?" I had been stewing and contemplating my options of escape, but they didn't need to know that.

A smile spread over Jase's lips, and it made me leery. "Let us make it up to you."

My eyes narrowed as I stared at him. "And just how do you plan to do that?"

"Since the Veil is now your home…"

I moaned a little too loudly, interrupting him. Four sets of eyes stared at me, and I shifted under their scrutiny, waiting for Jase to finish. *Way to make a spectacle, Olivia. This is your home now. Better get used to it.*

Zade took pity on me. "We thought you might like a tour, a chance to see the other regions."

My aggravation was forgotten as I sat a little straighter. "I would love that," I said, jumping at the opportunity to get out of the castle for a few hours.

"Good. You're not scared of heights, are you?" Kieran caught my gaze and winked.

What was he suggesting? "Depends if anything is trying to kill me."

Kieran swung his feet to the ground from his lounging position, a mischievous grin on his lips, and offered me a hand. "Let's go for a ride."

"I'll do it," the other three volunteered at once, causing Kieran to scowl.

Here we go again. This might not be a good idea, but I

was too tired to care. I just wanted to get out of the keep, and I'd been dying to see the rest of the Veil Isles, even with the ever-present dangers.

The dragons bickered among themselves while I sat by watching the madness. If a fight broke out in this little room, we'd be in trouble. There was only one way to solve this problem—drawing straws. I glanced around the room, looking for something to use, as I was pretty sure the Veil didn't have plastic straws. On an end table sat a bowl of colored stones, I pulled out four, and placed them in a hat I found on the coatrack.

"Quiet!" I yelled and waited for the room to calm down. I turned to Jase. "Close your eyes and choose a stone. The one who picks this stone wins." I held up a flat turquoise rock before sticking it in the hat with the others. He arched his brows. "Unless you don't want to…"

His eyes snapped shut before I finished, and he snatched one of the stones out of the hat, immediately looking at which one he had chosen, a pearly smooth gem. The disappointment in his violet eyes tugged at my heart.

Zade pushed off the wall and waited for me to hold up the hat before he too shut his eyes and chose a stone. The rock crumbled to bits of dust when he beheld it, his anger destroying the small pebble. I gave him a half smile and touched his arm. It bothered me when they were upset, especially on my behalf.

Kieran toyed with the hoop on his lip, giving me a lopsided grin. "I'm liking my odds." It was a fifty-fifty chance. Not wasting any time, the poison dragon selected one. He grinned like a total shithead, the silver in his lip glinting off the firelight. The turquoise stone proudly held between his fingers. "Come on, blondie. I'm going to take you on the ride of your lifetime."

Zade scowled.

Issik stood to his full height, eyeballing Kieran with his usual disdain.

Kieran's warm hand enveloped mine as he pulled me out of Jase's office, through the main hall, and into the garden. Once we were outside, he began to strip.

"A little warning would be nice before you go commando on me," I muttered under my breath as I turned around, giving him my back.

"You've already seen us naked," he pointed out.

I had. Multiple times actually, and I was positive I would continue to see them in all their naked glory. Lack of modesty probably came with being a shifter, but for me, it was going to take a lot of time to get used to it.

Kieran stood behind me and leaned over my shoulder, his breath in my ear. "You can turn around now."

"Are you naked?"

"If I said no, would you believe me?"

"No."

He chuckled, tickling the back of my neck.

I pursed my lips, keeping my back straight. "Are you going to shift, or just tease me all night?"

"Impatient, are you?" His voice washed over me with a different inflection, indicating he had started the process that turned him into a poison-breathing beast with scales.

Yes, I was impatient. I was dying for some fresh air and the chance to ride a dragon again. Who would say no? And this time, there would be no wraith to ruin the experience, or so I hoped. I waited a few more minutes before I turned around, and caught the tail end of Kieran's shift.

He was a magnificent dragon. They all were. Kieran's form wasn't as bulky as the others', but he was still large and powerful. Dark green scales papered over his body, growing lighter in color at the tips. He dropped his head in a bow, his emerald eyes glittering with humor.

Eagerly, I climbed onto Kieran's back, and ascended it without any struggle. He leaped off the terrace, and entered a dive toward the water. My stomach lurched as my breath caught. It was a thousand times better than any roller coaster at Great America. At the last second, before smacking into the murky sea, he used his wings to pull us up, letting his feet skim over the surface and creating a trail of waves in our wake.

Wrapping my arms around his neck, I squeezed my legs together. *Holy shit storm. I'm riding on the back of a dragon.* Never in a million years would I have thought this would be my life. We climbed higher, leaving the castle in the distance. A balmy breeze blew over my face, whipping my hair. His scales felt sleek and smooth under my hands.

"Better hang on." His voice instructed in my head.

I hadn't thought much about it the first time I'd been with Issik when he saved me—how he had the ability to communicate while in dragon form. I'd been far too overwhelmed and scared to wonder how it worked, but now I was curious.

"How are you able to talk to me?" My body was more relaxed, and I seemed to move with him as he glided and flapped his wings, alternating between the two.

Kieran's angular head tilted slightly to the side. *"I can project my thoughts into your mind."*

"Wow. That's amazing." And so was the Veil. Kieran took us over the lush forest that backed up to Jase's kingdom, and a flock of birds fluttered from the treetops, swirling around us. Deep in the center of the woods was the temple of their fathers, and where I'd been attacked. I shuddered at the memory, not keen to relive those moments.

"Look to the east. You will see Viperus Keep."

"That's your home?" I asked.

"It is. You will love it." Evident pride sounded in my head through his voice. He cherished his home.

The setting sun was at our backs, casting rays of pinks and oranges over the lower half of the sky. In the distance, just over a cluster of evergreens, rose a triangular tower—Viperus Keep. As we flew closer, the outline of a mossy castle came into view. Vines clung to the sides of the washed-out bricks, dangling below arched windows and off balconies.

"It's beautiful," I whispered in awe. Vegetation of all shapes and sizes surrounded the entire estate, from tall to short and fat to sparse.

"I will take you there soon, but for now, it isn't safe."

"Because of the wraiths?" I asked.

"They are only part of the danger."

Beyond the forest of Viperus, to the northwest, was unmistakably Issik's region. At first, it was just the change in climate that tipped me off. Whereas Jase's and Kieran's realms both had pleasant temperatures that reminded me of spring and fall, Issik's was a blast of icy cold air. The closer we flew to Iculon, the more arctic the air became, making it almost difficult to breathe.

My teeth chattered as I huddled deeper against Kieran's long body, using his heat to stay warm and insulated. "Is it always this cold here?" I asked, shivering. It brought back those not so pleasant memories of living on the streets of Chicago.

"Always. Do you feel how the air is thinner and harder to inhale? That's what it is like for Issik in our regions. His body needs the cold, just as Zade's thrives in the heat."

"Is it common for all dragons to have abilities like the four of you?" I inquired.

He chuckled. *"There is nothing common about us."*

I rolled my eyes. "I know that, but what about prior to the curse?"

"Before Tianna meddled with our lives, the Veil Isles brimmed with dragon shifters all with a kaleidoscope of dragon's breaths."

Kieran lifted us over a mountain, and deep in the valley below stood a majestic castle that looked as if it was made entirely out of glass. Frosty windows glowed a soft aqua, casting prisms of light onto the blanket of snow that covered every inch of the land. "It's like something from a fairytale," I murmured to myself.

"Don't let Issik hear you say that. He thinks Iculon is harsh and unruly."

A fond smirk tugged at the corner of my lips. He would think that. "What is the fifth region of the Veil like?" I remembered them mentioning a fifth dragon who had died while testing the strength of Tianna's curse.

"It is nothing but a barren wasteland, completely uninhabitable. Nature has taken over."

"What was his ability?" I asked, curious about the dragon shifter I'd never have the chance to meet.

"Influence." A sadness I hadn't meant to cause crept into Kieran's voice. I immediately sought to erase it. Rubbing my face against him, I pressed my lips to his neck. "I'm sorry," I said.

Underneath me, his body gave a deep exhale. *"He would have loved you."*

"Were the five of you always friends?" I wanted to take away the sudden pain I'd caused this usually lighthearted man.

Kieran's laugh was vibrant in my head. *"No. We grew up hating each other, seeing one another as rivals."*

It both was and wasn't hard to picture their relationship. At times, they were fiercely loyal, and at others, they fought like brothers. "What about now?"

"I would give my life to protect them." He projected the thought with intensity.

I believed him.

Without warning, he began to speed through the sky, our

surroundings a blur of pale blue and white. All I could do was hold on, and not get swept away by the rushing scene passing us by.

My eyes were unable to focus, so I didn't see what had him jetting off at first, but I sensed them. I wasn't sure how, but I knew the other three had joined us in the sky, other than by the quickening of my heart. I strained to peer through the flying strands of my hair and saw Jase and Zade on one side of us. Issik came up on the other.

"They just couldn't stay away." If dragons could scowl, Kieran was.

Yet, I didn't share Kieran's annoyance. In fact, I felt complete and bubbled with happiness.

My dragons.

There was no point in denying I wanted them to be mine anymore. They had quickly become a part of my life, and I wasn't going to let myself waffle on the issue again. "Can you blame them? Would you have stayed behind?" I asked.

He was silent for a moment, his formidable wings beating in the air. *"No. We all despise the curse that imprisons us, but we're proud of our homes and want to show them off."*

Only one region remained, Zade's, and I could tell he was excited.

Time went quickly as I enjoyed the thrill of flying. We left behind the cold and traded it in for an intense heat that had beads of sweat rolling between my breasts.

The Veil was so much bigger than my mind had drummed up. It was amazing how the land shifted from one climate to the next so seamlessly. White powdery snow gave way to charcoal ash. The earth became cracked and filled with a glowing stream of lava that ran from an active volcano, and a hazy cloud of gray smoke billowed from the opening at the top, trailing off into the air.

Of all the areas, this was the one that was the most

foreign to me and frightening. Fire was not my thing, but regardless of my fear, there was no denying its magnificence, like the dragon who lived here.

At the base of the volcano, surrounded by molten magma, was Zade's home. Made of obsidian, the castle pierced the sky with its sharp angles. There was nothing soft about the Crimson Kingdom.

My legs tightened around Kieran as he took a sharp right, tilting his body sideways. "You drop me and I'll come back from the dead to haunt you."

"Promise?" he teased.

I resisted the urge to kick him. He probably wouldn't have felt it anyway.

As we turned around, the sun was nearly gone and moonlight spread overhead, stars sparkling on the black water of Wakeland as we flew over. Jase's keep was in sight, and my heart sighed. From the sky, it looked lavish. Square towers rose up all in various heights with bluish-gray shingled peaks. A mystical mist hovered over the sea that bordered the castle on all sides, and an intricate bridge arched from the keep to the woods, connecting the home to land.

I'd become so enthralled by the glittering castle in twilight that I hadn't seen that we had company in the sky. It was Kieran who alerted me.

"Griffins," he hissed.

My head craned behind me, watching the dark figures descend upon my dragons. There were three of them—not as large as the descendants, but bigger than any bird on Earth. I was having a minor seizure. "What do they want?"

"You."

For the love of witches, could I get a break? "Let me guess. More friends of Tianna?"

Kieran dodged left, dipping his nose straight for Wakeland. *"You got it. Stay down, and no matter what happens, don't let go."*

Bracing myself, I latched my arms like a deranged monkey around Kieran's neck. Jase, Issik, and Zade flanked us on either side, and behind, forming a barrier around me. I couldn't believe these creatures really existed. Then again, I was riding a dragon. It shouldn't have seemed that farfetched, and I needed to learn to accept the outlandish.

One of the griffins managed to get directly above Kieran, and the ugly bastard raked the side of Kieran's back leg, causing him to stumble in the air.

"Kieran," I cried, but he quickly regained his composure. He was bleeding—not badly, but the sight had worry pitting in my stomach. "You're hurt."

"Don't stress. It is just a scratch, he reassured me."

Stress was my middle name.

My eyes scanned the skies, seeking out each of the dragons, and I exhaled when I counted three. They were safe, but we weren't out of danger yet. The griffins had rallied around Jase, circling him, and before the others had a chance to help, I watched as a nightmare unfolded.

In a uniform attack, the three birdy bastards expanded their spiny wings, and in a sonic scream that pierced my ears, they unleashed a fury of a thousand needles that shot from their feathers like a porcupine. The barbs embedded into the flesh of Jase's wings.

My heart stopped.

Without the use of his wings, Jase plummeted out of the sky, falling on his back toward the black water beneath us.

"Jase!" I bellowed, my voice echoing over the valley.

A tidal wave hit the shore as Jase's dragon form slammed into the water. I didn't think. I just acted, diving off Kieran's back straight into the dark ocean below.

My name was shouted in three different voices that grew distant as I plunged toward the sea. There were a million reasons why I shouldn't have jumped, including killing myself, but one reason overruled all the risks.

I had to save Jase.

It was ridiculous if I had taken a moment to really think about it. Me? Save a dragon? Laughable.

Splash! Cool, moon-bathed water rushed over my head. Frantically, I searched the murky sea for a large dragon flipping in circles. How hard could it be to find him? He was huge.

But Jase had shifted out of his scales and into his human skin. My heart quickened when I spotted him sinking farther into the depths of the ocean. I didn't hesitate, and started kicking as I dove deeper. The shoes on my feet flipped off, and I was thankful the dress I wore was lightweight, giving me the ability to move through the water.

Jase's body was limp. His head tilted forward. I didn't

want to consider what his lifeless form might mean. The only thought racing through my head was how fast I could get to him. Time seemed to slow, making each second feel like minutes, and I began to fear I wouldn't be able to save us both.

Finally, my fingers skimmed over his elbow, and I nearly cried. As I slipped my arms under his, I saw a flash of something shiny embedded in the seafloor. I gave it nothing more than a cursory glance, but for a brief second, I felt a magnetic tug, making my fingers twitch.

Swimming toward the surface, I prayed I'd be able to hold my breath long enough to get us there. In water, Jase's muscular form was a fraction of the weight it would have been on land, but still, it wasn't an easy feat—not for someone who was only a hundred and thirty pounds soaking wet.

My lungs screamed for air, and no matter how hard I kicked, it seemed as if I wasn't moving. Panic set in.

I was going to drown.

We both were going to drown.

Some hero I was. What had I been thinking jumping in after him? That was insane, and I'd never done anything like that in my life. I don't know what had come over me, but seeing Jase get hurt, fall, and be in real danger caused an impulse in me—a batshit crazy one.

Just when I thought I couldn't move my legs one more time, a pair of strong arms enveloped my waist. I twisted my head to the side, making out Issik's face through the cloudy water. His frosty eyes glowed an eerie blue. Another set of arms relieved me of Jase's weight. Kieran. I relaxed into Issik.

Halle-freaking-lujah. We're not going to die.

I broke through the surface and took a welcomed gulp of air. Water rained over my face as I shoved my hair out of the way. Issik's firm grip was still secured around my waist as he swam to the edge with Kieran and Jase alongside us.

Zade was waiting on the shore and pulled me out of the sea. "What the hell were you thinking?" he growled.

"Is he okay?" I questioned, panic raising the pitch of my voice.

Zade lifted a brow. "Jase?"

Duh. Who else would I be talking about? Unless someone else had gotten hurt, but no, they were all accounted for. I had made sure.

Zade's arms tightened around me, and he tugged me against his bare chest. I was shaking. "Relax, Olivia. He's all right."

My head shook. I couldn't. The adrenaline was leaving my body, and I wiggled out of his embrace, needing to see Jase for myself. Zade let me go, and I darted to where Jase was lying in the black sand and dropped down beside him. *Is he breathing? Why isn't he moving?* My hands roamed over his torso, feeling for a heartbeat, and my relief nearly jumped out of my chest when I felt a steady pulse under my palm.

Three shadows came to stand around me. "He's breathing," I whispered.

"It would take more than a band of griffins to kill a dragon," Zade retorted, as if it was preposterous to think Jase could have been injured or worse.

Glad to see that they were taking this seriously, but then again, maybe I was blowing it out of proportion and Jase hadn't been in real danger of dying. They did have a lifetime of experience. I knew nothing about dragons except for what I'd learned the last few weeks.

As I was scowling up at the three descendants towering over me, a hand laced its fingers with mine. My eyes flew to Jase's. He was awake and smirking at me. "Jase," I sighed, dropping my head to his shoulder.

"Your fear awoke me," he murmured.

I wasn't sure how that made me feel, but next to Jase being conscious, it took a backseat. "Don't you ever get hurt again," I ordered, poking a finger into his hard chest. "You scared the shit out of me."

"She's angry," Zade commented, sounding confused by my sudden change in emotions.

Nope. I wasn't even going to argue about him pointing out the obvious. "I'm sorry. It's just not every day I see one of my friends get attacked in the air." And I didn't want it to become a habit.

Jase sat up, water glistening off his abs in the moonlight. "You'll get used to it."

That was the thing. I didn't want to. My heart couldn't handle it. Look what happened during a minor incident. How would I react if something major did happen to one of them? I didn't want to think about it.

"What you did… jumping in after me… that was crazy."

My heart swelled. "Thanks. I think my craziness has been established, but I couldn't let you drown."

His electric violet eyes blazed into mine. "I don't ever want you to do something like that again. Do you understand?"

Water dripped all over the ground when I stood to my feet. "Last time I ever save your ass," I muttered, miffed I wasn't getting a thank you or *Geez, Olivia, that was so brave of you.*

"Promise me you won't do anything that reckless again."

I stared at him, giving him my stern eye. "Fine. I promise. But next time, it will be your life on the line."

Jase shook his head as if I was the most confounding female he'd ever met, and the other three snickered at me. I didn't even want to know what they found so funny because I was almost positive it was at my expense.

Zade's amber eyes flicked my way, running over my body. The fabric of my dress was plastered to my skin like a rubber glove, hugging my every curve. I might as well have been standing in front of them naked. His gaze finally settled on my face. "Let me dry you off."

I shivered, but it wasn't from the cold. I didn't tell him that. As Issik and Kieran gave Jase a hand up, Zade blew a gentle, toasty breath over my skin, evaporating the beads of water. It felt like being under a giant hairdryer.

Combing my fingers through my hair, I turned to see Kieran and Issik assisting Jase inside. He wasn't making it easy. The proud dragon kept trying to shake them off, but whether or not he wanted to admit it, the pin-sized wounds his body had sustained had taken their toll. He needed rest.

Maybe someone should douse him with some of his own tranquility.

The thought brought a ghost of a smile to my lips.

If there was one thing I'd learned today it was no matter how mesmerizing the Veil appeared from the outside, it was only a cloak to hide the darkness lurking within.

Harlow, Davina, and Kaytlyn were in the kitchen when I sauntered down in the middle of the night looking for a snack. I couldn't sleep, not after the excitement. All eyes swung to me as I interrupted their little girl powwow. The hushed whispers and muted giggles died.

And who could blame them?

I would have run from the room. I was a hot mess— bloodshot eyes, flushed cheeks, and wild hair. There was probably seaweed still tangled in it. I'd been too tired earlier to do anything but go to my room, but now there was nothing I wanted more than a long bath, a hot bowl of soup, and a marathon of Supernatural... in that order. But I would have to settle for the bath and soup. Sadly, Dean and Sam Winchester weren't in my foreseeable future—one of the things I definitely missed about Earth—TV. The Veil struggles were real. As was this mutual loathing between Harlow and me.

"What happened? Did you get into a fight with a barracuda?" the devil herself sneered.

"Something like that," I muttered, really not in the mood for Harlow's shit.

"I hope you plan on cleaning up your own mess," she snapped, leaning her back against the cabinets, her palms on the counter.

The other girls couldn't meet my eye and glanced away, staring at a bowl of fruit as if it was the most interesting thing in the world. I didn't blame them though. Staying off Harlow's radar was the smart thing to do.

I wasn't a smart girl.

It should be noted that I hadn't even opened the cooler where perishable food was stored. I hadn't made a mess yet. With bare feet, I padded across the kitchen and plucked a roll from a basket. "I thought that was why you were here," I replied sweetly, half anticipating an apple to be chucked at my head. It was a good thing there were no knives nearby because Harlow's face had turned bright red with rage.

Someone better step between us. A kitchen brawl was about to go down. The door to the kitchen flew open and in walked Issik. His eyes bounced between Harlow and me. "Is there a problem?" He directed the question at me.

Didn't anyone sleep around here? It had to have been well past midnight. Only a million problems came to mind in response to his inquiry. "No," I said. "Harlow was just offering to clean up after I eat."

Issik's lips almost cracked a smile. "Is that so?" he asked, knowing just as I did that Harlow would never offer such a selfless, kind gesture, but the glint in his eyes told me he approved of my wit.

I smiled. "We're all just one big happy family."

Harlow crossed her arms, glaring at me, but she didn't dare act out in front of Issik, and I stored away that little piece of information for later.

Issik grabbed a chunk off the bread in my hand and popped it into his mouth, hiding the grin that I knew wanted to part his lips. "Glad to see you're making friends."

Davina and Kaytlyn choked.

Dragging my smug butt out of the kitchen, I moved through the halls, leaving a trail of breadcrumbs behind me. I couldn't have cared less about attracting ants.

I wandered my way down the hall into the bathroom with a bounce in my step. Shoving the last bit of carbs into my mouth, I slipped off my clothes and sank into the bubbling square pool in the floor to wash away the faint lingering scent of salt and musk. Steam curled over the aqua waters, and a light glowed at the bottom.

Tucking myself into one of the rounded corners, I laid my head back and let the heat seep into my pores. Blonde tendrils of hair snaked over my shoulders, sticking to my skin. I don't know how long I stayed like that—at least an hour—but the water never turned cold. It was bliss.

Damn these long corridors and endless stairs. I just wanted to materialize in my room. Was that so much to ask for?

There was no one around to ask for directions—the castle asleep, as I should be—and if I ever found my room, I would fall directly into bed. I had more or less gotten the layout of the castle down in my head, but my brain had checked out, exhaustion finally creeping in. I was about to curl up on the floor and pass out.

The drafty halls were making me regret the decision to slip on a thin robe instead of something warmer. Gathering energy from somewhere deep inside me, I tackled the stairs. While grasping the railing as if it was my lifeline, I swung around the corner and barreled straight into Jase.

Talk about a sense of déjà vu.

His arms dashed out, landing on either side of my waist. For someone who'd been shot by a dozen darts and fallen from the sky, he was extremely steady. I leaned into him, drawing on his strength. "Why aren't you sleeping?" I asked, genuinely concerned as I looked up into his handsome face.

Lowering his arms, he watched me from beneath thick lashes. "I should be asking you that."

I sucked on my lower lip and glanced away. "Couldn't sleep. Too much excitement."

Those deep violet eyes were on mine; his brows pinched together. "What you did was reckless, but I think you understand how dangerous it was."

About as hazardous as being alone in a room with Jase, and the last thing I wanted in the middle of the night was a lecture, but it turned out we weren't alone.

"What are you two doing sneaking around the halls at this hour?" Kieran asked, stealthily coming up behind me.

The sound of his voice made me jump. "For dragons, you guys are pretty fucking quiet," I mumbled, my hand flying to my chest as my heart thumped wildly.

They rewarded me with twin smirks of wickedness, and neither of them wore a shirt. Why did they have to torture me like this?

"I was hungry," Kieran replied as if lurking around the castle in the middle of the night was an every evening occurrence. His eyes took in my apparel or lack thereof.

My nipples puckered at his slow perusal, especially when his gaze lingered at the exact spot I was hoping he wouldn't notice. I crossed my arms over my chest, trying to hide my breasts from making any more of a spectacle, but one glance at the two shifters and I could see a sudden desire churning within their eyes.

Holy smokes.

Jase's eyes bored into mine, and my cheeks flamed. "I'm starved. You, Kieran?" he tossed the question to him. Jase took a step closer, and the lopsided grin on his lips told me he knew what was going on inside me. It was a look that said food wasn't on his mind.

Hot Lips came up behind me with green fire in his eyes. "I've never been hungrier in my life."

What had gotten into them? Or better yet, into me? Why was I just standing there instead of telling them to back off? I wanted to blame it on my near-death experience and the surge of adrenaline, but it was mostly just them. *All* of them.

I glanced down the hall to make sure no one else was wandering around the castle. Jase's finger came under my chin, bringing my eyes back to his. Behind me, Kieran's hands landed on the side of my hips. I couldn't move and could barely breathe, wondering in anticipation what would happen next. Any confusion or uncertainty I had was quickly outweighed by my curiosity.

Kieran leaned forward, his even breath tickling my neck a moment before his lips brushed the sensitive spot. My head automatically tilted to the side, giving him more access. Jase pressed his finger to my lower lip, forcing them to part, and the heat in his eyes had my lower body clenching, tingles cascading inside me.

Those tingles exploded when he took possession of my mouth.

What is happening? Am I really making out with two guys? At the same time? My mind reeled from the smorgasbord of emotions rocking within me. Every hair on my neck stood up, and I worried one of them would stop... or wouldn't stop.

"Is this okay?" Jase murmured, taking the lead.

"I-I think so." I reached out and wrapped a single arm around Jase's neck; the other one laced through Kieran's fingers at my hip. The gesture wasn't lost on anyone. I wanted them both to stay just where they were.

"Olivia," Kieran whispered in my ear, causing me to tremble as his tongue flicked out.

I was sandwiched between them, my body somehow molded perfectly against both of theirs. Jase's skin smelled like the sea and Kieran's like the woods. I closed my eyes when their hands roamed over my body, slowly kneading my skin while pleasure seeped into my muscles.

Kieran's hot lips scraped over my shoulder, brushing aside the material. "You've been driving us crazy since you got here."

It felt like I was in cloud nine. What were they doing to me?

Covering my mouth with his, Jase deepened the kiss, sliding his tongue between my teeth as I moaned. Kieran's needy hands wandered down my body, sliding into the robe as his fingers splayed across my belly.

Oh my god.

My knees nearly buckled and might have if the two of them weren't pressed against me on either side. I couldn't stop my body from responding, arching so my breast rubbed Jase's chest and my butt nuzzled into Kieran.

It was too much. My body yearned for release, but here in the middle of the corridor where anyone could walk out was not how I pictured my first time. Would either of them care that I was a virgin? Should I say something and risk ruining the moment?

Kieran's fingers skimmed under the slopes of my breasts.

Nope.

Now was definitely not the time to bring it up.

Jase's lips moved from my mouth to drop kisses along my jawline. My eyes fluttered open, and over his shoulder, I caught sight of the three girls from the kitchen peeking at us through a cracked door. They all had stunned expressions on their faces, mouths agape, except for Harlow. She looked as if she wanted to tear my face off. The corners of my lips curved. I shouldn't be gloating. It wasn't my normal nature, but something about Harlow had turned me into a vindictive bitch.

It was clear she was jealous, that she wanted to be in the exact position I was—between two of the dragon descendants—but I wasn't willing to share, and I would fight her for them all.

Listen to yourself! my mind screamed. *They're not yours.* Not technically. Nothing had been discussed. So they kissed me. They desired me. But who was to say it would last? Who was to say they would be okay sharing me? It was hypocritical to expect exclusivity on their end when I wanted all four.

"Wait," I breathed, putting a hand on Jase's chest. He nipped at my earlobe before lifting his head to look at me questioningly. The girls closed the door they had been peering through, returning our privacy to us.

"What's wrong?" Kieran whispered, his lips brushing over my shoulder, making levelheaded thoughts impossible.

Other than I'd never done anything like this before in my life? "I don't want to just be another notch under your belts."

"That's not what this is," Jase assured me, and I wanted to believe him.

"You have an entire harem of girls living in your home," I reminded him.

"That may be, but most of them only work here. They have families of their own," he reasoned, dipping his head to silence me with a kiss.

"And the ones you've slept with?" I stopped him with the question.

Kieran snickered behind me.

I twisted to the side so I could glare at him too. "Same goes for you," I said, giving him a stern warning. "I might not have stepped foot inside Viperus Keep, but I hear the rumors about all of you. Issik might be the only descendant who doesn't have a reputation for being a slut."

"Did she just call us sluts?" Kieran asked with a smile.

"I'm being serious."

Jase forked his fingers into his messy hair, taking a step back from me. I immediately missed him. "I can see that," he replied.

"Maybe this wasn't a good idea," I muttered, dropping my hands and readjusting the robe to cover myself up. I clenched the material together at my neck.

Jase's lips pursed as the glimmer in his eyes faded. "This isn't why we brought you here. Seducing you was not part of the plan, and whether or not you believe me, you're not just another girl."

"There is something between us... between all of us," Kieran stated. "I think we're all curious about you."

I swallowed, feeling my body waver back toward them, but I stood rooted. "Maybe we can take things a little slower."

They both nodded. "We'd never do anything you weren't comfortable with," Kieran assured me.

"I appreciate that." What scared me was I was too comfortable with what we'd been doing. I didn't want to stop and might not have without the interruption from the three girls. "Good night, I guess."

The three of us awkwardly lingered for a few moments, uncertain what would happen next. I could see they both wanted to reach for me and pull me back into their arms. I wanted it too, more than I should admit. Biting down on my lip, I forced my legs to move and kept going until I was inside my room. Even behind the closed door and with them out of sight, it didn't diminish the strong desire in me. If they had followed me, I would have dragged them both inside and locked the door.

My brain no longer screamed at me to sleep, and after what had just happened with Kieran and Jase, I couldn't have anyway. The last thing I wanted to do was sit in my room replaying each touch and kiss we'd shared. It would drive me straight back into their arms.

In the days that followed, I saw very little of the descendants, and even though I told myself not to let my feelings get hurt, they were. Sure they were busy dragons, doing whatever dragons did, but without any friends in the keep, I was lonely… and bored.

I could only sit in my room and count the stars in the mural or wander aimlessly about the castle so many times. It would drive even the sanest person insane. I also wasn't the sanest person to begin with, so the going insane thing happened quicker for me. To pass the hours, my mind took it upon itself to come up with excuses for their absence.

Were they deliberately ignoring me?

Why would they do that?

Was everything they had said to me about being special a lie?

Was I being tossed aside like all the other girls?

To hell with that! If they thought they could kiss and ditch me, they had another thing coming. Dragons or not, their scaly asses were grass.

Were they secretly planning something they didn't want me to know about?

I stopped wearing out the wood floor in my room from pacing and strode to the door with purpose. Before I crossed the threshold, I glanced down at my attire to make sure I wasn't half naked. There would be no more wandering the halls in flimsy robes.

The door swung open viciously as I stormed out to hunt down the dragons, but as I rounded the corner, I found someone else. Harlow. The wicked grin on her cherry lips was all trouble.

For the love of peanut butter, I couldn't take any more drama. "Harlow, I'm not in the mood to mince words with you." I tried to pass her by, seeing as there wasn't a dragon in sight and that's whom I sought.

"You slut!" she hurled at me.

So much for being the bigger person, and walking away. I paused and took a breath before I turned around and faced her. "I'm sorry. I didn't know you had the authority to judge me."

Her hand flew back as if she was going to slap me, but I stared her down, daring her to touch me. "They'll get tired of you. They always do," she spat, her hand suspended in the air.

My gaze shifted to the left, staring at her open palm. "And let me guess, you'll be there to comfort whichever dragon will have you. I've got news for you, *sista*. I'm not giving them up. We have a connection you'd never understand."

Her face turned red. Not a pretty look. "You're nothing but trash. I heard they found you on the streets."

The fact that she knew that hurt. It meant one of them had talked about me to her, and I didn't like being discussed behind my back, especially with someone like the bitch-monster herself. But I refused to let her get to me. I lifted my chin. "In order for you to insult me, I'd have to value your opinion, which I don't."

"You little—"

I'd had enough name-calling for one day. I snapped my hand closed in front of her face. "Zip it. Now, get out of my way before I do something you'll regret." I jerked away and took a deep, cleansing breath that did nothing to stop the tremors of rage.

I should have known better than to turn my back on a girl like Harlow. In high school, Tracie Wilson had it out for me because she thought I had flirted with her boyfriend. So not true, but the point was Tracie had believed it. I had brushed her off and ended up flat on my face in the hallway with a split lip. She had shoved me when I turned my back on her. You think I would have learned my lesson.

Barely taking two steps, I felt a hand fist into my long hair and yank. Pain radiated from my scalp. I tried to steady myself and failed, pulled back like a ragdoll. I was going to kick her ass as soon as I got my claws on her.

Blindly swiping through the air, I attacked, just waiting for my hands to make impact, and once they did, I dug in, using my nails on her flesh. "What is your deal with me? What did I ever do to you?" I hissed, twisting her arm, and she released the fistful of my hair.

Her eyes were narrowed and filled with hate. "Before you came here, I was the one they came to."

Propelled by pride and fury, I took one long stride toward her. "Why you conceited, self-absorbed little—" Clumsy because of the ferocity of my temper, I missed my target, which had been her pretty face, and managed to spin in a circle. Not my finest moment, but then again, I'd never been much of a fighter.

I did, however, end up pinning her to the floor. So what if I accidentally fell into her, knocking us both down? It still counted. She went wild underneath me, scratching like a feral cat over my arms and face. There was definitely blood under her fingernails—my blood.

With a feral growl, I grabbed her wrists and stuck my knee into her gut, but I swear, she must have been a wrestler in a prior life. Girl had moves I couldn't even fathom. Swinging her leg into some kind of pretzel knot around my shoulders, she put me into a chokehold.

Oh my god. We're going to kill each other.

My face was turning purple when a pair of strong arms enclosed around my waist, pulling me off the she-devil, but Harlow wasn't finished with me. She came flying to her feet as I fought against my restraints. A cold chill sent tremors through me.

"Touch her and you'll deal with me," a hard voice said behind me. It was Issik.

Of all the descendants to see me in such a state, it would have to be the frosty one. He was the only one who hadn't warmed up to me, and still, I felt something between us when we were alone.

"Relax, little warrior. She won't hurt you," he whispered in my ear.

I reached for calmness and concentrated on the coolness radiating from him. The fight went out of me, and I sunk against Issik's firm body.

Harlow straightened. Her eyes shot daggers at Issik in an epic stare down. I had no doubt who would win. Issik had a severity about him that trumped Harlow's bitchiness. "Jase will hear about this," she threatened us.

"Yes, he will... from me," Issik assured her, not the least bit intimidated by her warning.

She flinched. "If you care so much for her, why don't you do us all a favor and take her to Iculon?" she challenged him, still trying to figure out a way to get rid of me.

"For someone who is so bright, a lot of dumb things come out of your mouth. That's not how this works, and you know it, Harlow." He said her name with a sharp bite.

"But she isn't the one," she argued, relentless as always. It made her sound like a petulant child.

Issik's hands loosened around my waist so that they held me out of comfort versus restraint, trusting me not to punch her in the boobs. "You know nothing of the curse. It still remains to be seen if Olivia is who we've been searching for. And it would be wise for you to remember your place in Jase's kingdom. The liberties he has allowed you will quickly end if you lay a hand on her again."

She huffed. "How dare you speak to me like that!"

"I think it's time you retired to your room. You've done enough damage for one day." I didn't miss the tension in his voice.

The second Harlow stomped her ass out of the hall I spun to face Issik. "Are you really going to tell Jase what happened here?" My voice quivered, fighting the tears that suddenly threatened to spill over my cheeks.

"Hey, don't do that." He brushed the pad of his thumb under both of my eyes, wiping away the water that had gathered there.

"Sorry. I hate crying."

"After the last few days you've had, no one would blame you," he said, keeping his voice low and leveled.

I sniffed, forcing the lump back down my throat. "I don't think I can do this." Everything felt so gloom and doom. I wasn't strong enough. I wasn't the one. They were all going to die because I couldn't break some idiotic curse cast by a jealous witch.

"Yes, you can. If you can jump off a dragon's back, in mid-flight, straight into Wakeland Sea, you can stick this out a little longer."

"I wish it were that simple." How I felt at the moment was anything but badass. I felt like a failure, and all I wanted to do was pack up my shit and go home. Screw the Veil. I didn't need this crap.

Issik kept me in his arms, allowing me to indulge myself in the cry fest of the century. If Harlow could see me now, she would have eaten up weakness. I let the bully win.

Through a haze of tears, I stared up at Issik. "Sorry about your shirt," I said, having left behind a big wet spot, but at least he'd been wearing one.

His eyes frosted over as he stared at a spot on my cheek. "She hurt you." The sound of his voice was strained, and he gently touched the raw scratch.

I shrugged, wary of the darkness I saw churning in his eyes like a blistering winter storm. "It's nothing. I'm fine."

"You don't think Jase should know that Harlow is causing problems?" he asked, his brows drawn together in confusion, but curiosity was there too.

"I don't want to add more stress to the situation. You guys have enough to deal with. This is something Harlow and I need to work out ourselves."

I couldn't make out the expression on his face, but that was typical when it came to Issik. "What did you do to get on her bad side?"

"Breathe," I replied dryly.

His lips cracked at the corners into what looked like a grin.

"Did you just smirk?" I teased him.

"No, definitely not." His lips returned to a thin line, but I could see he struggled to hold it in place.

Tucking my hair behind my ears, I shifted my weight to one side. "Just admit it. You find me amusing."

"I will admit no such thing, but if it takes the sadness from your eyes, then it might have been the smallest of smiles."

I beamed. "I knew it. You actually like me."

"So, are you going to tell me what happened between the two of you, or am I going to have to torture it out of you?" He wouldn't dare, and we both knew it—nothing but empty threats from Ice Prince, except in Harlow's case. Then he had been dead serious.

"She's had it out for me since I arrived." I avoided telling him about what happened to gain Harlow's wrath—the kiss with Jase and Kieran. What a kiss it had been. My mind was still reeling, and my emotions were a mess. I didn't want to go there. "I went to, um…" My brain searched for a plausible excuse. "…get something to eat and she cornered me. Started calling me names." That was as much of the truth as he would get.

His jaw twitched once, and I could see he was fighting back the urge to press me. "I told Jase he shouldn't mess around with Harlow. In case you haven't figured it out, she was sleeping with him, but he ended things before you got here, and hasn't touched her in weeks. She's jealous of you. Just a warning: be careful around her. I don't trust her. Never have."

Processing what I already knew about Jase's relationship with Harlow, I nodded, and ignored the pang in my chest.

This was the longest conversation Issik and I had ever had. What he said made sense, regardless of the fact that I didn't want to feel sympathy for her. I could understand Harlow's anger at Jase for suddenly ignoring her. It would put me in a not so pleasant mood, but I'd like to think I wouldn't act as she had. I would go straight to the source and ask what his deal was.

"Did you ever get to eat?" Issik asked.

"No." I answered, shaking my head. "The wrestling kind of killed my appetite."

"A good fight always makes me hungry."

"Does that include girl-on-girl fights?" I was razzing him, and it came naturally.

His eyes twinkled, and this time, there was no mistaking the smirk that spread across his lips. "Nah, that's a different kind of hunger, little warrior." He draped an arm over my shoulder. "Come on, I can't have you starving to death."

My lips twitched as I rested my head on his chest, letting him lead the way. I didn't expect him to take me to his room, only one of the million surprises I'd had recently, and I'd completely forgotten the reason I'd been in the hall in the first place.

Dinner wasn't anything fancy, but there was wine and candles. We sat on the floor with the terrace doors open, revealing a sky filled with glittering silver stars, which provided all the light we needed. The room was cool, but in a refreshing way, and we gorged ourselves on crackers and cheese. I drank the wine, but only one glass, and we talked for hours. There was so much more to the quiet shifter than I'd imagined.

I'd never been much of a drinker and sipped the smooth, cranberry liquid slowly. That was all it took to cause my eyes to become heavy. Feeling peaceful, my lips loosened, and I gave in to the questions that had been on my mind. "Do you have anyone waiting for you at home?" I asked Issik.

"Are you asking me if I have a girlfriend? No." He shook his head, his light blond hair falling around his jawline. "Iculon is a cruel and unforgiving land. Not many can withstand the constant brutal weather."

My heart grew sad for him. No wonder he was rigid and reserved. He had no one to care for him.

The coolness of his fingers brushed along my cheeks, seeping into my skin. "Don't feel sad for me, little warrior. I prefer to live alone."

Did he really though? How did he know if he had never

shared his life with another person? "I think I would like to live in an ice castle," I murmured, my eyes blinking very slowly as my voice drifted off.

Soft lips pressed against my temple. "I would keep you warm," I thought he whispered, but the wine got the better of me, and right before I dropped off into a deep slumber, I recalled the reason I had left my room—damn dragons.

~

The sound of deep voices dancing around me woke me up—four of them to be exact. What were the descendants doing in my room?

And then I remembered I wasn't in my room, but Issik's. I must have fallen asleep. Oops. My cheek pressed against a pillow, and a thick blanket draped over my body. The smell of Issik's crisp scent lingered on the bed, and I found it comforting, unlike the dragon himself. Keeping still and my eyes closed, I tuned into the whispered conversation that was growing in volume.

"Did you sleep with her?" a low voice asked that I was seventy-five percent sure was Kieran's.

"No," Issik said with an edge. "But would it have mattered if I had?"

"Yes!" came three hisses.

A moment of silence followed, and I held my breath. "What is going on? It's been decades since we've fought. And never over a girl," Jase said.

I couldn't believe they were talking about me. Scratch that. Yes, I could. Arguing over me seemed to be a pastime they partook in frequently.

"We've never all desired the same girl before," Zade commented.

"There is that," Jase added. It sounded as if he was pacing the room.

"It must mean something because it's clear we all feel something for her," Kieran voiced.

"So what are we going to do about it?" the fiery golden god wanted to know.

"For starters, we need to put all our energy into figuring out what we're missing. Time is ticking by, and seducing Olivia is not going to give us our freedom, or save us from extinction," Jase lectured them, doing what he did best—leading.

A bunch of groans and shuffling feet responded, but eventually, there were grunts of agreement.

Don't I deserve a say in the matter?

"What's the plan? Do we have any leads? Something to tell us what direction to be searching in?" Issik asked.

A frustrated sigh resounded around the room. Jase. "We've been over every inch of this island, scoured every book in the kingdoms, tracked down every person with an ounce of magic, who are now all dead. What's left?"

"We have five months left to figure it out," Issik reminded him, not that any of them could forget about the sand quickly slipping through the hourglass.

"And five months to keep Olivia alive," Jase added. A cloud of foreboding lingered in the air.

"How hard can that be?" Kieran asked, in an attempt to lighten the bleakness that had settled in the room.

"Tianna's curse is complex, as we've learned. The closer we get, the more danger she will be in," Dimples explained.

"We can handle it," Zade reassured, sounding determined and confident.

"But can she?" Jase interceded.

"I think she can." Issik spoke up. "She's tougher than she looks."

Hell yes, I was, and I loved him for sticking up for me. We had shared a sincere moment last night, and it was nice to feel as if someone believed in me, even a little bit.

"With us by her side, we can take on whatever Tianna throws at us," Zade vowed with fervor.

"But that doesn't mean we can't be more careful. Mistakes cost lives," Jase reminded them, lowering his tone.

"I don't like this," Issik said, and I felt his eyes move over my pretending-to-sleep form.

"None of us do, but this is the only way. Enough is enough. We must end this curse no matter what," Zade retorted.

"I agree," Kieran's voice was determined. "But I'm not willing to risk Olivia's life for my own. We've lived more than a hundred years. She's only had seventeen."

"Even if it means it is the end of dragons?" Jase asked.

"The world already thinks we're fiction..." Issik let his thought dangle.

"Then we all agree?" Jase asked, waiting for someone to speak up.

I was dying to open my eyes just to take a quick peek to see what was going on. Were they nodding in agreement, shaking hands, or something else entirely? How would I know if they would forsake their lives for mine if I couldn't see them? And did I want them to?

I wasn't sure.

I had plunged into a lake from several feet up in the air to save one of them.

"How long have you been listening, Cupcake?" Jase asked.

Gulp.

Wrinkles spread over my nose, as I pried one eye open. "Not long." Sighing, I gave up the pretense of sleep. "Just something about the curse, less kissing, and blah, blah, blah."

Jase's lips twitched. "So everything."

I shrugged. "Maybe. What happened before Issik said he didn't sleep with me?"

A scowl settled on Issik's eyes, while the other three tried to maintain their unaffected postures. I don't know why they pretended with me. I could see right through each of them. They weren't as tough as they appeared.

Jase leaned against the far wall, faking an expression of consideration. "I think we were talking about how much trouble you are."

Grabbing a pillow from the bed, I chucked it across the room, not caring which dragon I hit, as long as I hit one of them. "You brought me here. Don't forget that part."

"She has a point," Zade agreed.

Of course I did. The pillow thumped to the floor, not hitting a single one of them. Wow. Pitiful.

A hint of a smile danced on Issik's lips as he sat at the end of the bed. "I guess there is no need to catch you up, little warrior."

Slowly, I sat up, keeping the blanket in my lap. "Next time, try not talking about me when I'm in the room, sleeping or awake."

Jase gave a quick nod. "Noted."

My eyes narrowed, making the rounds to each one. "Is there going to be a next time?"

"That we talk about you? Definitely." Kieran grinned.

Humor shone Zade's eyes as he stared at me from his spot in the corner. He was sitting in the only chair, his long legs stretching out in front of him. "You're stuck with us. We're not leaving your side."

That shouldn't have made me crazy happy, but it did.

"I think we need to hug it out," Kieran offered. A mischievous gleam that was ever present in his eyes glimmered.

My arms spread wide, letting a grin cross my own lips. "Group hug," I announced, singing it in a high-pitched tone.

The four shifters only wasted a single heartbeat before bombarding me on the bed, even Issik, the coldest dragon of them all, and I suddenly found myself engulfed in the world's sexiest hug as they all tried to wrap their arms around me. The bed groaned under the additional weight, and I thought for sure it would collapse.

In that moment, surrounded by the descendants, I didn't care what anyone else thought. They were mine.

"What happened to your face?" Zade demanded, seeing the red mark courteous of Harlow.

My eyes moved to meet Issik's and I swallowed. I had a feeling lots of roaring would be echoing in the castle.

When they had said they weren't leaving my side, I shouldn't have taken it literally, because in the next few days, they vanished—all four of them.

Again.

The descendants were proving to be the worst protectors in history. Every time one of them took off, they had a million reasons why I couldn't tag along. It was pathetic. I understood they were worried I would get hurt, but being trapped inside the castle day in and day out wasn't good for my mental health, which was just as important. I couldn't possibly help them break the curse if I had mush for brains.

I hated being left alone. I hated being apart from them. I hated feeling sorry for myself, which was exactly what I was doing.

Pity party for one, please.

My foot connected with the innocent rock and I watched it skip over the dirt path of the courtyard. It was good thing cell phones didn't work in the Veil, or I'd be blowing up theirs.

I avoided every part of the keep Harlow could possibly be in, and that really limited me to my room. Since our little hair pulling, nail scratching spat, we'd both been steering clear of each other like a plate of brussels sprouts. Neither of us had apologized, and I was definitely not going to make the first move. She had it coming. I wasn't sorry for my actions.

The grounds were fairly quiet today, everyone taking care of their daily responsibilities. I waved at Eve, the gardener, who was tirelessly trying to maintain the over-grown hedges surrounding the castle. The flowers and plants in the Veil seemed to grow at an alarming rate. Everything was bigger here, kind of like Texas. Raven, a sweet, shy elderly lady, gathered a bouquet of flowers for inside the dining hall, as usual. She didn't live in the castle, but in a small home on the edge of the woods bordering Wakeland. She had been one of the chosen girls many,

many years ago and stayed, making a life here in the Veil Isles.

Continuing to stroll along the path that circled the keep, I enjoyed the sun on my face. A lazy cat wound its way in between my legs as I walked, keeping me company. Petra, I thought her name was—one of a few strays that hung around the kitchen waiting for Milly, the cook, to toss them scraps, which she did each day.

There was a routine to life in the Veil that I found comforting, yet mundane, and the existence I'd had before the kidnapping began to feel like it had happened to a different person. They were separate; one didn't bleed into the other, and I wanted to keep it that way. The girl from before, she didn't exist here.

Dropping down off the dock onto a small section of sand, I kicked off my shoes and sunk my feet into the tiny grains warmed by the sun's rays. A tender breeze blew in from off the sea, flirting with the hem of my dress.

My eyes were drawn to the sky, hoping to catch sight of the dark outline of a dragon. I don't know how long I stood in there, staring into the vast turquoise sky. Too long. Eventually, I sat down at the water's edge and hugged my knees up to my chest.

"*Olivia Campbell...*" someone whispered my name.

My gaze went to the aqua waters. I don't know what I expected to see, but there was nothing, only the gentle waves, a few fish, and lots of seaweed.

Am I hearing things?

To be safe, I scanned the area to make sure I was truly alone and Harlow wasn't screwing with me. There was no one around, and yet I couldn't shake the feeling that I was being watched as an inkling of unease snaked down my spine.

It was strange. Today the sea lacked its usual fogginess.

The color of the endless sky reflected in the waves, allowing me to see into its depths. At home, Mom and I used to go to the beach every weekend during the summer, and sitting here now on the edge of the water, feet dangling just under the surface, I thought of her, of how much I missed her.

What would she think of my life now?

Would she approve of the descendants? Of dragon shifters?

The idea brought a tiny smile to my lips.

I highly doubted that when Mom thought of my future, she would have envisioned me entangled with four guys. And I know for a fact she wouldn't have believed in dragons.

Speaking of missing someone, it was awfully silent with the four of them gone. I hated it. I knew they had responsibilities and a curse to break, but I would have gladly helped, and it would have been much preferred to doing nothing.

My reflection stared back at me over the placid waters. My long, honey-colored hair fell over my shoulders, and as I leaned closer, the ends dipped into the sea. At first glance, I didn't recognize myself. My aqua eyes lacked the fear I'd gotten used to seeing in them when I was alone. My lips seemed naturally pinker and my cheeks peachier. I attributed it to the lighting, the glow of the sun giving my skin a dewy quality.

Have I changed that much since I've been here?

It wasn't solely my physical appearance, but also how I felt inside. I was different... older and wiser; that sounded so cliché, yet it didn't make it any less true.

"Olivia." The soft voice of a woman sounded again.

What the fuckity-fuck?

Okay, this time I wasn't imagining voices. Someone was trying to get my attention, and after the second eerie call, I was all ears. Problem was, I had no idea where it came from.

And then I saw something in the water.

It wasn't *something* I saw in the water, but *someone*, a woman rising from the bottom of the sea. I blinked and blinked again, convinced the sun and the reflection of the water was playing tricks on me.

Zade's warning about the sea and the creatures that lived in its depths echoed in my head. Sirens. Loch Ness monster. Things I probably couldn't imagine. Surely, what I was seeing was a mermaid, but her body was more fluid than solid.

She stayed under the surface, staring at me with white eyes that glowed like an oracle's. I found them freaky and struggled to look at them. Her vibrant red hair floated around her heart-shaped face in a tangle of waves.

"Olivia," she whispered my name again, but her mouth never moved. Her eyes fixated on mine. Her words transported into my mind. *"Let me help you."*

I couldn't believe I was talking to a woman of the water. "How?" I asked, unwilling to blindly accept some strange woman's aid. She could be dead for all I knew, or a siren trying to trick me.

"I have what you seek."

I shifted up onto my legs, my knees tucked beneath me. "What is it you think I'm looking for?"

She laughed, a melodic and airy sound like spring showers. *"What everyone on this island wants, to break the curse."*

"What do I need?" My heart quickened in my chest.

"I must show you," she insisted.

Did I look stupid? Were the letters s-u-c-k-e-r written across my forehead? "Let me guess. I need to swim in there," I said dryly, pointing to the sea.

Her head nodded up and down, causing her hair to float out behind her. *"It's the only way."*

Said every crazy person ever. My eyes roamed over the water, contemplating if I was insane enough to jump in. I already knew the answer because I had leaped in to save Jase, but now there was no one around to save me. "Why should I trust you?"

"Do you have any other options?"

Point taken. But that didn't mean I liked it. "Who are you?"

"My identity isn't important. What matters is you have something none of the others had."

"What do I have?" I asked.

Her eyes grew frantic. *"You must hurry. The sun is setting, and without the light, we will lose our opportunity."*

She was evading my questions, but I wasn't sure it really mattered who, or what she was. If there was even the slimmest of chances I could break the spell, or find something to help us, didn't I have to take it? Would Jase, Kieran, Zade, or Issik do the same?

They would without hesitation.

I had to do it.

"I'm so going to regret this," I muttered as I glanced down and grimaced. The mysterious woman had faded back into the dark parts of the sea, leaving the decision up to me whether I followed or not. I nibbled on my lip. The sun shone at my face, hitting the water, and that was when I saw it—the spark of something shiny.

What is that?

There was definitely something down there other than the mermaid, and it wanted me to find it. I don't know how I knew that; I just did.

I felt torn between taking a swim—I'd been warned to stay out of the water—or returning to the keep, and forgetting about the shiny object and the woman. There were so many reasons to not go after it. What if I drowned? I was a decent swimmer, but still, I didn't know how deep the water was. What if I was attacked? There were things in the lake I never wanted to come face to face with.

Shit.

Quickly scanning the grounds to make sure no one was around, I grabbed the hem of the slim dress I wore and lifted it over my head, leaving me in just my undergarments. I dipped my toes in and shimmied toward a set of rocks, dividing my attention between my own stability and glaring into the water.

It was dark, but not so dark that I couldn't distinguish between the grayish water and the gritty sand on the bottom.

You're fine. You can do this. Just swim down. Grab the pretty item. And get out. Easy peasy. You lived on the streets. How much scarier can a body of water be than that?

With all that nonsense chattering in my head, I held my breath and plucked up my courage, plunging into the sea. Water rushed over my head, gliding smoothly along my skin. I opened my eyes, giving myself a second to adjust, and kicking my feet, I dove onward toward the glittering object. My movements were jerky and graceless.

When something brushed the side of my leg, I tried to keep my cool but I couldn't repress the shudder. *Don't think about it. Just focus on reaching the bottom. Get in and get out.*

Pursing my lips, I stretched out my hand, ignoring the burning in my lungs, and the ache in my legs. I was so close. Just another few inches. The water around me rolled, and I realized with a jolt of panic that I wasn't alone in there anymore.

Please, don't let me get eaten.

I didn't let myself think about the dark shadow approaching me, and kept my focus on the object. A hum vibrated in my ears, and just as my fingertips touched the smooth surface of the translucent stone, another set of fingers brushed over mine.

My eyes glanced up.

Jase? What was he doing in the water?

All rational thoughts went out the window.

A thousand pinpricks sank into my body as a burst of colored lights haloed through the water like a disco ball. It came from the stone. Jase's hand clasped over mine, securing the rock between our joined fingers.

I gasped, inhaling a stream of water, and Jase reacted, wrapping his arms around my waist and launching us to the surface three times as fast as I could. Breaking through the water, I coughed, sputtering seawater from my nose and mouth.

A fresh wave slammed up against me, but before I could go under again, Jase lifted me out of the ocean and onto the dock. Coughing up the last bit of water, I collapsed on my back, eternally grateful to be back on land.

"What the hell were you thinking?" Jase yelled, barely giving me a second to catch my breath. "I told you to stay out of the sea."

He was beginning to sound like a broken record, which wasn't wholly his fault. I pushed myself upright, meeting his unhappy gaze. "That I could do something other than sitting around on my ass."

He drew in a ragged breath. "And swimming was the first thing that came to mind?"

"No."

"What were you doing then? You could have drowned."

Thank you, captain obvious. It was then I remembered the stone in my hand. My eyes traveled to my palm, staring at the glittering glass stone. It was smooth, serene, and lightweight. "I went to get this," I said, holding up the crystal that was purple in color, just like his eyes.

"A rock? Now I know you are nuts."

"I don't think it's just any stone," I said, unable to take my eyes off it. A pulsing rhythm thudded where it touched my skin as if it had a heartbeat. This was what the mysterious water woman had wanted me to find. She had led me to it.

"Let me see it." Jase's hand reached for the crystal, and that was when shit got psychedelic.

I swore the world stopped as a prism of light shimmered violet, dancing behind my eyes. The vibrant blend of blue and purple burst, threading around Jase and me, encircling us in a bubble of moonbeams. Our hands were connected with the stone between them.

My eyes immediately sought out his, and I gasped. I recognized his dragon, seeing the fierce creature that lived within him staring back at me. A surge of energy pierced my heart, and I braced myself for the searing hot pain I was sure would follow. But there was only pure stillness. It bloomed in the center of my chest, spreading to every point in my body—every muscle, every bone, every hair follicle. It wasn't just a feeling of tranquility; it was as if I *was* tranquility.

The swirling colors intensified to the point I worried about going blind. It built and built until... *boom*. They burst like a grenade blowing up a rainbow. Jase's eyes widened in horror as my name exploded in a roar from his lips, but it narrowly registered in my brain until his arms wrapped around me, shielding me from the flash. My face was plastered to his bare chest, and I thought, *I am going to die*. At least it would be in Jase's arms.

Not a horrible way to go.

For a few minutes, I remained still. I stayed planted against Jase, waiting out the wave of mystical energy. My legs trembled, but I didn't worry. Jase was there to keep me from falling. I was almost afraid to open my eyes, preferring the darkness to the dazzling colors.

"Olivia," he whispered, his gentle fingers coming to rest on my cheeks.

I blinked a few times, testing the brightness. Being blinded once was enough for me. "What just happened?" I asked, tilting my head upward.

The muscles in his shoulders tensed. "That rock isn't just a pretty piece of glass. I don't know why I didn't recognize it."

The stone—that was twice now that we'd touched it together, and made fireworks fly. Wiggling to put a little bit of space between us, I lifted my hand and spread open my fingers. I eyed the round purple crystal. "What is it?"

"The Star of Tranquility."

He reached to touch it again, and I snapped my fingers closed. His hand was suspended in midair as his eyes sought mine. A light of understanding dawned in them. Strange things happened when we both touched it, so for now, I'd hold on to it.

"It was lost during the Great War. Each descendant had a stone crafted by the gods, representing their power. They were embedded in the crowns of our forefathers, passed down through the generations, but they haven't been seen since the Great War when our ancestors were struck down. We all assumed they had been destroyed." His fingers dove into his damp hair, his mind traveling back in time.

"Does it have any magical properties?" I asked. Considering what just happened and, even now, the stone humming with energy it seemed likely.

Jase arched a brow. "It's been so long since I heard the stories, but it was rumored the gods enchanted the stones with fire, ice, tranquility, poison, and influence, giving the very first dragons their powers."

I couldn't imagine having such an amazing history, and to think I held the source of his power in my hand, this tiny little stone. "I'm assuming it hasn't lost any juice," I said, locking eyes with him.

"Do you feel any different?" he asked me, his stunning features darkening.

"I don't know. Should I-I?" I chattered, a shiver rolling through me, but as the words left my lips, I truly took a moment to take stock of how I felt from the inside out. I sucked in a deep breath, noticing a flutter stir in my chest. *What is that?* It didn't seem like a big deal and could have easily been from nearly drowning.

Retrieving his discarded shirt from the dock, he tugged it over my head, and I wiggled my arms into the sleeves. The material was warm and smelled like Jase. "It's hard to say, but I'm sure we will find out soon enough. The stones don't appear to have lost their abilities."

"I'll say," I muttered.

"We're going to talk about how stupid it was for you to jump into the water like that, but first, let me look at you." He took a step back as his eyes gave me a critical once-over from head to toe. The firmness crossing his brows softened, and I took that to mean I hadn't grown a second head or a third arm.

The sudden frown that grew on his lips spiked a bout of doubt, but he no longer looked at me. Jase rotated his wrists from left to right, staring at them with an expression of wonderment and disbelief. "It can't be!"

"What can't be? Because I definitely felt some weird magical mojo a minute ago."

"You did it!"

"What did I do?" I asked, squinting my eyes as I tried to see what I was missing.

"My bands… they're gone."

A funny look contorted my face. "What bands?" I prodded. Getting information from him was worse than going to Target on Black Friday.

A strangled laugh erupted out of him. "The ones that keep me locked to the island."

"Oh," I said. How had I not noticed them? Maybe they hadn't been physical bands, but some kind of magical ones. "Does that mean the curse is broken?"

"I-I'm not sure," he stammered. The man never stuttered. "We need to find the others," he announced, grabbing my hand without the stone.

I had to jog to keep up with him. We passed around the back of the castle and through the courtyard, barging in through the double doors. Kieran, Zade, and Issik were in the hall, sitting at the oversized rectangular table. Strands of wet hair clung to the back of my neck, dripping water down my spine.

The three dragon shifters stopped what they were doing

and flipped their gazes to Jase and me. "What's wrong? Why are you both soaking wet?" Issik asked.

"You were supposed to find her, not drown her," Zade said, his tone dry and slightly annoyed.

Jase sat me down in one of the empty chairs. "I found her all right. At the bottom of the sea."

Three sets of eyes regarded me with disapproval. "Did she fall in?" Kieran asked, probably assuming I had.

Jase folded his arms and shook his head, enjoying the retelling a little too much. "No, I saw her jump."

He did, huh? "I went to get this," I butted in, throwing out my hand on the table so they could all see the Star of Tranquility.

Silence greeted me but was shortly followed by…

"Is that…?"

"It can't be."

"Holy shit."

Three different responses, but they all shared the same incredulity.

"It's the Star of Tranquility," Jase said, his violet eyes illuminating with the same glow as the crystal as if they recognized each other.

Kieran leaned closer to inspect the stone. "How? I thought—"

"We all did," Jase interjected. "But she didn't just locate the lost stone. Something happened when we both touched it. Look." He shoved out his wrists for the other dragons to inspect what obviously my human eyes couldn't see.

Their eyes volleyed from Jase to his hands and back again. Zade's brows scrunched together as he grabbed Jase's arms, turning them back and forth, much like Jase had earlier. "They're gone."

"The stone removed them. I felt it but wasn't sure at first."

Darkness crept over Jase's face. "You still have yours," he said to the three dragons who were like brothers to him.

"Which means the curse isn't broken," Issik's powerful voice concluded, putting a dark veil over our short-lived elation.

Disappointment crashed inside me, and I rubbed the heel of my hand over my heart.

"That's exactly how we all feel, little warrior," Issik said, sensing my desolation for them. It hovered over all of us like a thick, black, ugly storm cloud.

"I don't understand. Why didn't it lift the curse?" Desperation laced my voice.

No one said anything, the silence thickened around us.

"Because we don't have all the stones." Issik announced, finally putting together the pieces. "There were originally five crafted. If the Star of Tranquility survived, it's possible so did the others."

"We need to find them," Kieran surmised.

Issik nodded in agreement.

"And I'm guessing you guys have no idea where to look." It had been purely accidental, stumbling upon the rock... or had it? The water woman. She had led me to the stone, but who was she? How could I summon and enlist her help again? I wasn't sure why I hadn't told them about her.

Zade heaved a heavy sigh. "They could be anywhere. The isles are quite large."

Having recently seen it with my own eyes, I could attest to the sheer size of the Veil. "It will be like finding a pot of gold at the end of the rainbow." I added to the gloom. Nearly impossible.

"For fuck's sake," Zade swore under his breath.

"But we have to try," I said, pleading with each one of them as I looked them in the eyes one by one.

Jase had both palms flattened on the table. "And we have less than five months to do it," he reminded.

Talk about a time crunch.

Silence followed.

None of us expected the sound of a female voice laughing in a husky, flirty tone, brimming with mockery. It came from all directions, surrounding us. My first thought was Harlow, but the pitch of the tone was wrong, raspier.

All four of the descendants bristled and shot to their feet, rushing into the courtyard. The expressions on their faces were murderous. I followed behind them, refusing to be left alone. They stood in a fierce line, strong and unified. I felt sorry for the idiot dumb enough to challenge them all.

I lifted up on the tips of my toes, trying to see over their broad shoulders. It wasn't easy, but I managed to find a hole in between Issik and Zade and weaseled my way in. A woman with flaming hair was poised in the gardens, a billow of white smoke at her feet, making it hard to tell if she actually touched the ground.

From my obscured view, her piercing gaze found mine. "You didn't think it would be that easy, did you?"

For an instant, a terrifying instant, there was only the sound of the sea and the wind and my own heart pounding. *Is she talking to me?*

A wisp of unease curled over me. I shivered and huddled back into Issik, instinctually knowing who the voice belonged to. He wrapped me in his arms, but the cold that settled into my chest wasn't from Ice Prince.

"Tianna," all four dragons hissed together, identical dark scowls marring their handsome faces.

Tianna?

The bitch finally came to show her face.

If I could get a firm grip on reality, I'd choke it. I felt as if the world had been spinning since I jumped into the sea, maybe even before then, and I couldn't catch my balance.

Panic embraced me.

What does she want? Can she hurt me? Hurt the descendants? Can they hurt her?

Question after question tumbled like rapid-fire bullets in my head. There was something eerily familiar about the witch.

The witch's lips curled into a grin. "So you finally found one of the keys. Took you long enough. I was beginning to think you'd given up."

"Never," Issik growled, his hands dropping from my back and fisting at his sides.

Every muscle in Jase's body was coiled and ready to strike. "Time isn't up yet."

Tianna pinned her gaze on him with a look of pure hatred. "No, you can still fail. And fail you will." Her hand lashed out and caught fire, lighting up her face in a green glow.

A knot of fear balled in the pit of my stomach. My hand clutched Issik's arm, needing someone to keep me safe. I should have grabbed Jase. A dose of his calming nature would be divine right now.

My movement had Tianna turning toward me, a place I didn't want her to look. What I wanted was to be invisible. "Such a plain human."

I should have been insulted but that would imply I cared what Tianna thought about me, and I didn't. She was the source of all my recent problems, the reason I had been kidnapped and brought to the Veil. Or maybe I should have thanked her. Without the curse, I never would have learned about dragons or met the descendants, and now I couldn't imagine my life without them.

167

"I'd rather be plain than a vindictive bitch." Oops. The words just came tumbling out of my mouth. I should have thought about it before I opened my trap because she had powers.

But I had dragons.

Four of them.

I won.

Tianna lost her shit. With a flick of her wrist, she cast a flame of energy in my direction. Kieran threw himself in front of me, opening his mouth and blowing out a blast of emerald smoke. Poison expelled from him, fizzling out the sphere of fire.

"Pathetic," she laughed. "I've waited and grown weary of watching you through the curtain of magic as you fail time and time again, doomed to make the same mistakes."

Under my hand, Issik's arm flexed. The ice dragon was dying to freeze her lofty ass. "I'm assuming there's a point to this spontaneous visit?" Issik asked.

"I've come for the star," she stated as if we were all dim-witted peons. Lightning struck, the sky suddenly as black as Tianna's heart.

Jase's cool gaze switched from Tianna to me. "Is that what this has been about?"

"Whatever you do, Olivia, don't give her the stone," Kieran whispered into my ear.

This was something about they all seemed to be in agreement. My fingers tightened over the smooth rock.

With unblinking eyes, she let a long moment pass. "Did you honestly think I cared about any of you? You have always been a means to an end. Sure, I had a little fun, but the games are over. Now, give me the stone, and I'll let your little pet live."

Only, by coming here and exposing her desire for the descendants' stars, she had revealed a weakness. Did her greedy heart want power so much she would destroy an entire race to gain it?

In Tianna's case, the answer was a big fat yes.

Holy shit. At Tianna's threat on my life, all eight of the descendants' eyes shone brightly with large, colored pupils.

"No. Not going to happen," Jase snarled, his voice reaching a low note I'd never heard before in a guy. It was more animal than human.

Tianna waved her magic-happy hand in the air, disregarding them like children. "Don't be foolish. It's the only way you can get the freedom you so desperately want."

"You've already cursed us. What more do we have to lose?" Kieran snapped.

"Her," Tianna hissed.

A wall of dragons formed around me. "Touch a hair on her head and you won't get what you want." Issik's words dripped below freezing temps.

Rage like I'd never seen before erupted from Jase, deep and vicious. "Trust me, we'll find a way to make sure we kill you."

"Are you willing to take the chance that I won't kill her?" Tianna tilted her head to the side, giving them a moment to ponder, not that any of the dragons needed time to think on it. "In case you need a reminder of how serious I can be…" She called a creature down from the sky to perch on her arm, skimming her fingertips over the ruffled feathers of its face. The griffin was about the size of a crow. She whispered in its ear, "It's time they heard you scream, dearie."

"Get her out of here!" Kieran yelled.

A ring of orange fire materialized, boxing us in. She threw her head back and laughed. "Not so fast. Olivia and I need to have a little girl time. You boys don't mind, do you?"

"Hell yes, we mind," Zade roared, his amber eyes flaming.

"You're not getting anywhere near her." Issik shifted into

J.L WEIL

his alternate self beside me, not bothering to remove his clothes. His dragon loomed over us—glorious, fierce, and very pissed off. A stream of snow spouted from him, extinguishing the flames.

Kieran transformed next, following Ice Prince's lead. Jase and Zade framed me in between their bodies.

From above us, more griffins attacked, diving down at my dragons, their claws jabbing into the fleshy part of Kieran and Issik's wings, but they didn't show an ounce of pain. Using his tail, Kieran smacked one of Tianna's pets, sending the odd, bird-like creature sailing through the air and into the sea.

Jase looked at me, worry present in his eyes. It was then I finally saw it.

Fear.

He was afraid for me. Tianna had already cursed them, but she could use me to hurt my dragons. I wasn't going to let that happen.

"Olivia. Go. Now!" Jase bellowed, ducking as Tianna tossed another of her famous fireballs she was so fond of using.

All I could think was *I need to run*, and I begged my legs to work, but they were rooted to the ground. God, I was going to be sick.

I opened my mouth to scream, but no sound came out. Instead, a hazy, purplish mist I'd seen before expelled from deep inside me, rising up my throat and puffing into the air.

Tranquility.

How the hell had I done that?

The fighting stopped, and the Veil became eerily quiet for a few prolonged heartbeats. Everyone stared at me, except for the griffins. The feathery creatures were lying on the ground, sleeping.

I had done that.

"You!" Tianna hissed.

Uh-oh. She had on her ugly face, and I was in deep shit.

The air suddenly shifted, turning the dark sky foggy. Out over the sea, the winds picked up speed, morphing into a wicked twister, headed straight for me. Damn the witch.

"Olivia!"

"Olivia!"

"Olivia!"

"Olivia!"

Four voices bellowed, but they couldn't save me.

I was swept up in the tornado of magic Tianna had created, which twisted me off my feet and away from my dragons. I lost all sense of the world as I spun and spun in the center of the cyclone, Tianna's laugh echoing in my head like nails on a chalkboard. When my feet touched the ground, I was disorientated, my eyes unable to focus.

"Oh, come the frick on," I mumbled, my hands stretching out in the air to ground myself before I tipped over. I could tell I had been transported somewhere, but my brain was still too muddled from the trip.

"You're quite a funny human," Tianna's voice said in front of me.

I focused on the blur of red through all the muted colors of green, knowing it was the witch. *Where am I?* It could be nowhere good. Tianna stood in the middle of a forest as tall and powerful as any goddess, and maybe that was how she saw herself. With her arms thrown high, eyes glowing white, her fingers spit out tiny sparks of silver electricity.

"You're going to have to kill me," I said with a voice far steadier than I felt inside. My knees were trembling, and my stomach was still rolling.

She smiled coldly. "That is still an option, but I'm hoping more of your blood won't be spilled."

My stomach clenched in raw terror. "You need me to get the other stones, don't you?"

Her hands settled on her hips, sparks of energy still crackling from them. "What if I do?"

"Why me?" I asked.

"That's simple. Because they all desire you. You accepted them, not loving one more than the other, but the four of them equally."

It was true. I did care about them all. Love might be a far stretch, but really? This was the grand reason I was the key? Talk about a letdown. I'd been hoping for something dramatic. Special powers. An ancient lineage. Fireworks.

This couldn't be happening. How was I going to get out of here alive without handing over the very thing that would give the witch more power?

Tianna summoned a ragged-edged dagger. "Hand me the stone, an I'll go away… for the time being. I won't hurt you."

Like hell, she wouldn't.

I couldn't take my eyes off the dagger. It wasn't simply steel. Magic pulsed through the blade, etched into symbols I didn't understand. My pulse roared in my ears, and before I had a chance to doubt myself, I turned and ran. I didn't expect to get far. There was no moonlight to guide me, and I plunged heedlessly into the dark forest. I fled through the trees, my legs vibrating as I dashed down a slope. I was so blind with fear that I didn't see Issik's dragon until I rammed into him.

Relief poured through me. I was safe, right? The others would be here in moments.

Then it all happened so fast.

Issik let out a roar that echoed over the Isles—pure rage. He opened his mouth, expelling an icy mist of blue at Tianna, but the witch always had a plan. It was then I remembered the dagger in her hand. She cocked back her arm and let the blade go.

The sudden wheezing I heard left me confused. My frantic gaze searched for Issik. There in his chest was Tianna's dagger. A dragon's scales should have been impenetrable, but the magic imbued in the blade gave it the power to impale even the strongest of defenses. At the sight of blood, a strangled gasp parted my lips. She had hit one of my dragons.

NO!

Being so distraught over Issik's injury, it didn't register that I had been hit as well, but not with a magical sword. Issik's frost had struck me in the heart after he'd been stabbed.

I sucked in a sharp breath. Never had I been so cold in my entire life. It knocked the wind out of me, and all I thought was death couldn't be this painful.

"I will see you soon," Tianna's voice whispered in my ear, and then I was falling, as if from a great height.

"Olivia!" Issik shifted and somehow managed to catch me before I hit the ground.

Black spots danced behind my eyes, and then there was nothing.

Fire burned in my chest as I came to. The heat inside me exploded, pulsing in a giant wave that ran through my blood. It rippled like a solar flare straight from the sun.

With effort, I peeled my eyes open, and the first face I saw was Zade's hovering above me.

Holy shit. I'm not dead.

"This better be the last time I have to breathe fire into you, little gem."

"Is she gone?" I croaked, my throat feeling like I'd swallowed barbwire.

Zade nodded. "She vanished just as the rest of us showed up."

My relief was overwhelming, but I also knew it would be short-lived. Her promise echoed in my ears. She would be back. Her desire for the stones would keep her hunting and threatening me. Then I remembered I wasn't the only one who'd gotten hurt.

"Issik, he was stabbed. Is he okay?" I tried to sit up, but Zade pressed back my shoulders, keeping me on the ground.

"Not so fast," he scolded me. "You need a moment to let your body return to its normal temperature."

Didn't he understand? I didn't care about how hot or cold I was. If Issik was hurt, bleeding, we had to—

Issik sunk down to his knees beside me, his head resting near my face, but not too close, as if he was afraid to touch me. "You're alive," he whispered.

I blinked. What a silly thought. "Me? I'm not the one who got stabbed."

There was so much regret in his eyes, and it hurt my heart to see it there because of me. "I could have killed you."

"But you didn't. And it wasn't your fault," I stressed. "She threw a knife at you."

His blond brows furrowed together. "I never should have been so careless. Not with you, little warrior."

Kieran and Jase shuffled their feet behind us then, and I sat up slowly. "What's wrong? Why are the two of you so antsy?"

"Do you have it?" Jase asked, crouching down beside Issik.

The fingers curled around my palm slowly opened to show them the Star of Tranquility. It glittered under the starlight, vibrant and clear. It was safe. And so was I. Well, mostly. There was still the crazy thing that had happened when I screamed, but I was ninety-nine percent sure the cool stone in my hand was responsible for that.

A heartbeat later I found myself plastered against Issik's chest. "I'm so sorry. I thought we lost you." A look passed from him to me, and I squeezed him tightly, needing comfort as much as he did.

Pulling back, my eyes connected with his bright icy eyes. "Turns out I'm not that easy to kill, especially when I have four dragons around to save me."

Kieran lifted me off Issik and spun me around in his arms. "We'll always be here to protect you," he vowed.

I was counting on it, for I knew we hadn't seen the last of Tianna. We needed time to regroup, as did she, and next time we'd be ready for her.

To be Continued...

DRAGON DESCENDANTS

A REVERSE HAREM SERIES

A NOTE FROM THE AUTHOR

Thank you so much for reading Stealing Tranquility, Dragon Descendants, book 1.

I truly hope you have enjoyed reading it, if you have, please show your support by leaving a review. It only takes few moments, visit my Amazon Author page:

J.L. Weil
https://amzn.to/2OPz6J3

Olivia's and the descendants' journey continues in Absorbing Poison, Dragon Descendants, book 2

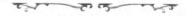

For the latest news about new releases, sales, upcoming books, giveaways, and more join my news letter today!
http://www.jlweil.com/vip-readers

DRAGON
DESCENDANTS
SCHOOL OF
A REVERSE HAREM SERIES

ABOUT THE AUTHOR

USA TODAY Bestselling author J.L. Weil lives in Illinois where she writes Teen & New Adult Paranormal Romances about spunky, smart mouth girls who always wind up in dire situations. For every sassy girl, there is an equally mouthwatering, overprotective guy. Of course, there is lots of kissing. And stuff.

An admitted addict to Love Pink clothes, raspberry mochas from Starbucks, and Jensen Ackles. She loves gushing about books and Supernatural with her readers.

She is the author of the International Bestselling Raven & Divisa series.

Don't forget to follow her!

www.jlweil.com
www.facebook.com/jenniferlweil
www.twitter.com/JLWeil
www.instagram.com/jlweil

Made in the USA
Monee, IL
02 August 2021